THE BLACKMAIL MACHINE

THE
BLACKMAIL
MACHINE

by *Felice Holman*

Illustrated by Victoria de Larrea

COLLIER BOOKS, NEW YORK, NEW YORK
COLLIER-MACMILLAN PUBLISHERS, LONDON

The Blackmail Machine is also published in a
hardcover edition by The Macmillan Company

Printed in the United States of America

First Collier Books Edition 1973

1 2 3 4 5 6 7 8 9 10

For
Nanine, Gina,
Toni, Gail,
Bruce, Sally, Janet,
Liz, Sue, Chris,
Adam, Jerry,
Jimmy, Karl, Paul,
Nadia, Rita, Victor,
Beth, Benedict, and Miles,
who are getting ready
to take care of it themselves.

Contents

THE BLACKMAIL MACHINE

1

An Unidentified Flying Object

Early on a Saturday morning toward the end of July, a tree house with several children aboard was first seen flying or hovering just above the cornstalks of Mr. Manoover's farm; then it flew off over the orchard.

When Mr. Manoover ran to tell his wife, she looked at the clock over the stove, sniffed the air, and said tightly, "Shame on you, Sam Manoover . . . and at this hour of the day!" And then she went back to stirring a pot on the stove. Mr. Manoover, who, in fact, had been making a regular check of his medicinal spirits (to make sure they were not spoiled by the summer heat), began to wonder if he had seen what he had seen, and left the kitchen in a hurry.

A little later, the tree house, motivated by something

no one on the ground quite agreed on, was seen over the Goodbury town park. It was low—just a bit above the trees—and, since it moved slowly, it was possible to identify some of the passengers. One of them was Arabella Serafin. A child playing on one of the park swings recognized her while he was on the upswing, and ran to tell his mother. "It's got nothing to do with us," she said, turning the page of her magazine. "Go back and get your swing before someone grabs it."

Shortly before noon, Mrs. Serafin, standing at her kitchen window, wondering where Arabella had been since breakfast, looked up when she heard a kind of whirring. It seemed to her a shadow was crossing the garden. Her glasses were steamed, so she wiped them, but the shadow was, indeed, there. And then she caught sight of something above the birch trees.

"My word!" she exclaimed to her husband. "That looks just like Oggy Clay's tree house. What in the world is it doing so close to our birches?" And then she started to tremble. The tree house was *moving!* Slowly it crossed the birches and hovered over the center of Mrs. Serafin's rose garden. Mrs. Serafin wiped her hands on the dish towel and ran out into the garden, followed closely by Mr. Serafin. Shading their eyes and squinting against the sun, they could see that there was no question about it. Oggy Clay's tree house, always firmly anchored in the next yard, was now somehow set loose and floating over their heads. There seemed to be quite a few children on it. One of them was Arabella!

"Arabella!" Mrs. Serafin screamed—screamed because now she was half out of her mind with worry and something or other in the tree house was making a terrible racket. "Arabella, what *are* you doing! Haven't I told you never to go away without telling me where you are going?"

Arabella unfolded her long legs and stood up. She came to the railing and waved—a cool and reserved wave, not an enthusiastic wave.

"Arabella!" screamed Mrs. Serafin. "Come down! Come down this instant. Children! All of you! Come down. That's very dangerous."

Arabella leaned over the railing, causing Mrs. Serafin's heart nearly to stop. "No," called Arabella. "No, I'm sorry, Mother. We can't come down right now. We just came by to let you know we are quite all right, so you won't worry."

"Won't worry!" exclaimed Mr. Serafin.

"Will you tell the other parents, please?" Arabella went on. "The Kitts, the Clays, the Roses, and the Ambassador from Peroque."

"Arabella," cried Mr. Serafin, "what is the meaning of this? What is it you want?"

But the tree house was moving away now, veering off toward the east and moving across the meadow toward the river and the woods. In a few minutes it was out of sight.

What was happening!

To discover this it will be necessary to go back just a bit.

2

Arabella, Murk, Melinda, and Oggy

By the time she was eleven Arabella Serafin was quite used to being exceptional. At first, it is true, it had been amusing being the center of attention. It had been diverting, for example, to read aloud to the grown-ups when she was four, although they never seemed really to pay attention to the stories but would just gasp and say, "Just *listen* to her; she can read *every* word!" "Of course I can read every word," Arabella would think. "What on earth would be the good of reading every *other* word?" But she kept silent.

It wasn't long, however, before she was beginning to wish they would stop hanging over her shoulder. They kept asking her and asking her, and she just didn't have the time. There was entirely too much to read to waste her time showing off. She had been neglecting her reading in the sciences because her reading in history was taking most of her time. She took her extraordinary erudition for granted, without pride or snobbishness, and wore it with the ease of a well-fitted hat. The other children in the neighborhood were used to Arabella, and she was a handy source of information. "She's just like me," Melinda Rose once said. "Just like me, only *much* smarter," and she added, "and not as . . . well . . . pretty." And there *were* gaps: Arabella spoke no language but English, and as for mathematics, she left that for school —it gave her something to do there. Because *that* was another thing! They made her go to school, and it was utter nonsense. Even though they skipped her a grade it was a terrible bore. She daydreamed, she fell asleep, and while the teachers admitted that her test grades were superior, she rated very poorly in deportment and class participation. The teachers complained that she wandered from the subject when answering, or, more often, didn't answer at all because she didn't seem to hear the question.

"Bound the state of Michigan, Arabella," Miss Prilly would say. "Arabella! Michigan!"

"Michigan!" Arabella would be thinking. "Imagine, it's only three hundred years ago that Etienne Brulé discovered the falls of the St. Marys River! A mere three hundred years in the whole long history of mankind!" And that led her to think of other waterfalls; and that made her think of her favorite falls, Laughing Whitefish.

"Arabella!" the teacher would cry. "*What* is the answer, please?"

"Laughing Whitefish!" Arabella would say confidently, going back to her daydreaming.

There was someone else in the classroom who seldom answered correctly, and that was Maurice Kitt—called Murk. Murk *heard* the questions all right, but he just didn't know the answers. And that was because he didn't study, and that was because he had only one real interest, which was motors. Not once—not one single time—did the teacher ask him a question about motors. If she had she would have been surprised. There was hardly anything about motors that Murk didn't know. He had learned a great deal from his late grandfather, who had started fooling around with motors over fifty years ago. The shed in the yard of

Murk's house was filled with stuff his grandfather had been working on—automobile motors, engines he had been inventing, and even the remains of his attempts to make an airplane, which just didn't quite fly.

For the rest, Murk gathered his knowledge nearly every day in the town junkyard. There, with the patience of a true connoisseur, he collected the parts that wasteful citizens discarded—a bolt here, a nut here, a spring, a pin, a bit of wire, a transformer, a condenser, a spark plug, a bearing—absolutely anything. These things he brought home and cleaned, mended, and oiled, and kept in beautiful order in his grandfather's old shed; and eventually he assembled them into motors that really worked.

But then he would be sitting in class, thinking of a certain kind of bearing that he needed for a motor he was working on, and a voice would say, "Bound the state of Michigan, Maurice." And Murk would think, "Michigan is where Detroit is, where they make all the automobiles." But if he tried to bound it, he could see Michigan completely surrounded by beautiful antique motor cars. He would close his eyes and conjure up a vision of a marvelous old Hupmobile followed by a splendid Model A Ford.

"Maurice!" Miss Prilly would exclaim. "What *are* you thinking about?"

"A Stutz Bearcat," Murk would say, since truthfulness was another of his good qualities.

And then, to avoid complete frustration, the teacher, wild-eyed, would turn for succor to Melinda Rose, because when it came to bounding states of the Union, there was no one more reliable than Melinda Rose. She would arise from her chair, smooth her starched skirt, toss her lovely chestnut hair, smile endearingly, and recite the boundaries of the state of Michigan in a tone and with a reverence usually reserved for poetry or prayer. When she was through, the state was as neatly packaged as a Christmas gift.

"Thank you, Melinda," the teacher would say, and sinking gratefully into her seat, that poor woman would reach into her desk for a lump of sugar and announce recess.

Out on the playground, Arabella always came alive fast. First she would do two or three forward handsprings to get her blood circulating, and then five or six backflips. When she began to tingle, she would shoot over into a corner of the playground, throw her-

self on a grassy bank, and whip out whatever book
she was reading. Just now—just before the end of
spring term—she was going over the Trojan War, at
the same time reading modern European history to
give her perspective. Occasionally she would look up
from her book and watch the playground games.
They were interesting but somehow not as appealing
as the book. Besides, you could lose. Arabella did not
like to lose.

Murk, as usual, sought out a game of one o' cat, and on the June day we are talking about, Melinda went looking for her next-door neighbor, Oggy Clay. She had something special to discuss with him. Even if he was a bit younger, and sometimes crabby, Oggy had a special attraction—he was the proprietor of the best tree house in the town of Goodbury, in the county of Meredith, in the entire state, on the entire east coast, and possibly in all the United States.

It was about the tree house that Melinda wanted to see him. Melinda Rose was expecting a visitor in a short time and she wanted to bring her visitor up into the tree house. She wished, therefore, to ask Oggy to invite her guest, since this was, after all, Oggy's right as sole owner of the marvelous tree house. Moreover, Melinda wished to offer her services in the cleaning and sprucing up of the house, since her visitor was a Very Very Important Person—ZoZo Sejura, the young son of the new Ambassador from Peroque.

Melinda tried to explain to Oggy how it all came about. "See, my father was in Peroque last year, because he's in the sugar business, you know. Well, Mr. Sejura—he wasn't Ambassador just then, he was something to do with sugar—well, he was very friendly to my father, and he showed him all over Peroque, and he had my father stay at his house and meet his wife and his little boy. And that's ZoZo.

"Now, you see, Mr. Sejura is going to be the new Ambassador, and he is coming to the United States in a few weeks, and he is going to stay with us for the weekend until his house is ready in Washington. And, well, I'm very excited because they are Very Important People."

"Well, sure," said Oggy, seeming to consider the matter. "You can bring him up if you want to. I invite him." Because Oggy was really quite as confident as any king of a fairly elegant castle that there was no visitor too important for his tree house.

3

Hot, and Getting Hotter

The first few days of vacation were full of the kind of time-filling do-nothingness that is so exciting and satisfying and so full of the promise of summer's endless freedom.

Arabella read a volume of Socrates and a volume of Winston Churchill. Murk tinkered with the motors that needed tinkering with, without needing to take time out to go to school. Melinda, in preparation for the Very Important Visit, tidied up everything in her room, shined her party pumps, and started practicing curtsies before the long mirror. There was no telling when she might be called upon to bob one. Oggy Clay varnished the deck of the tree house, mended a shingle on the roof, and tested the knots of the rope ladder.

Then he would spend an hour or so up there playing the oboe. He didn't leave the garden; his mother liked to know where he was.

But by the end of the first week of vacation, Arabella made a discovery. While she had always felt that unlimited time to read was all she really wanted, she discovered the need to turn more and more handsprings and flip more and more backflips, and then, after all, that did not seem quite the thing. So she started wandering about the house. It was hot.

"It's hot," Arabella said to her mother.

"Of course it's hot," said her mother reasonably. "It's summer."

"But in the summer we should be on our vacation," said Arabella. "When *will* our vacation be?"

"We're not sure yet, dear," said her mother. "Father is unusually busy in the city. It may not be until the end of August."

"But it's hot!" said Arabella, sticking to her point.

"Don't nag, Arabella."

"Well, I think it is debasing for Father to put off his vacation. He is trapped in a mesh of meaningless routines and compulsions that civilization has imposed on us."

"Oh, Arabella!" said Mrs. Serafin sadly. "That's not a very nice way to talk about your father. He is a most conscientious man, and it's just that a man in his position has duties and routines. Certain things are just expected of a man like your father, you know."

"That's just what I said," said Arabella, slamming the door as she went out to see if anyone was about. "Honestly! Grown-ups!"

Melinda Rose was beginning to feel the suspense of waiting for her visitors. There were still a few days to go before their expected arrival, and her mother was a nervous custodian. She wouldn't let anyone walk on the freshly waxed dining room floor, touch the polished mirrors, or sit on the velvet sofa. Indeed, Mrs. Rose seemed to have nothing else on her mind. At the moment, having bobbed three hundred and forty-five curtsies, Melinda had full confidence that she was the fastest curtsy-bobber in Goodbury. And while she could scarcely bear to admit it to herself, she was nearly fed up with it. The trouble with grown-ups was that they started talking about things too soon and then you couldn't stand the waiting. She decided to go and see what was doing in the neighborhood.

The shed where Murk worked on his motors had a tin roof, and when the heat of the summer day started to reach a peak, Mrs. Kitt called, "Murk, why don't you get out of that hot shed and get some fresh air?"

Murk stepped out and looked at the blue sky and found it attractive. As he shut the shed door, he complained to himself, "But if I had been lying around in the shade on the lawn, she would have said to me, 'Murk, don't you have anything to *do?*' Grown-ups!" And Murk stretched and decided to go and see where everyone was.

Everyone was at Oggy Clay's tree house, and a generally restless and dissatisfied group it was. Melinda was saying, ". . . and they keep saying, 'Be careful, don't track up the floor,' and 'Don't rumple it,' and they're so busy getting ready for the company that they don't have any time for a person."

And Oggy was saying, "And my mother says, 'Oggy, can't you stop playing that oboe long enough to let me hear myself think!' And then the next day she says, 'Oggy, you're not neglecting practicing your oboe, are you?' Gee!" And to underline his distress he improvised a few furious arpeggios.

"Ooooooo!" exclaimed Arabella, exasperation building in her with the heat of the day. "Really, it is sometimes impossible to understand what motivates grown-ups. Most of the time they miss the point entirely. They seem to have everything backward. For example, my father is working in the city today. Today, when the temperature is ninety-three!"

"I know," said Murk. "Mine is, too. But they have to earn a living, see."

"Of course," said Arabella, "but it's just the system . . . an arbitrary system. Why do we always have to do things according to a system? Why couldn't they, for instance, all have a vacation every day the temperature goes over ninety? After all, things don't fall

apart when people take Sundays off . . . or if there
is a terrible snowstorm and no one can go to work.
Are people afraid to change things? Or maybe they
don't even think about it!"

"That's it," said Oggy. "Like I tell my mother I'm
old enough to go *anywhere* by myself, but . . ."

"Now then, school!" said Arabella, warming to
her subject. "*There* is a really mixed-up idea that
adults have! 'What are the exports of Venezuela, Arabella?' Here I am, panting—positively panting—to
learn things, and what do they want to teach me?
The exports of Venezuela! Do you realize what we
could learn in the time it takes to look up the exports
of Venezuela?"

"What?" asked Melinda.

"Well, the factors contributing to the decline of the
Roman Empire, for example."

"Is that better?" asked Melinda.

"Infinitely," replied Arabella. "No comparison.
And, of course, if you have time left over, you can
learn the exports of Venezuela, if you're interested."

"But why do you want to read so much history,
Arabella?" asked Oggy.

"Well," said Arabella, "because it's all written down
there—everything they did. What they did that was

wonderful and what they did that was terrible. All the wonderful and terrible things. And you can read it and say to yourself about something, 'That was right, and look at all the good it did.' And then you can say, 'How *could* they have done that? Why did it happen that way?' And all the time, you are sitting way up high above it, and it doesn't really . . . doesn't really . . . touch you."

"But that's all over," Oggy said impatiently. "*Now* is what's important. Seeing what there is to see now is what's important."

"Of course, now is important," said Arabella. "But history is important, too, and it isn't as . . . as . . ." Arabella stared off over the treetops. "As scary," she finished softly.

Oggy perked up. "Hey, are *you* scared, Arabella?"

"Well, sometimes," Arabella said. "Sometimes, but not when I'm reading."

"I'm not scared of anything," said Oggy.

Arabella stopped staring and threw the crossword puzzle at Oggy.

"Well, anyway," said Murk, "you're right. They don't teach us what we want to know. Take motors. They don't teach you a thing about them. I have to find it all out myself."

"And they tell you you're not old enough to do it yourself, and then they don't show you how!" Oggy was beginning to get caught up in the spirit of the occasion. "And cauliflower!" he added. "How do grown-ups get the idea that stuff is to eat? Anyone can see, just to look at it, that it isn't."

"*I* like cauliflower," said Melinda.

"Oh, *that* sort of thing!" said Arabella. "That sort of thing is just a matter of taste. But it's when you look around and see the whole system . . . honestly! It's hard to believe that the world is run by grown-up people!

"And the really maddening thing is," Arabella went on, "that *we* are so helpless. *They* run everything! *They* decide things! *They* tell us what to do, and we can't do *anything!*" She became carried away. "Here we are," she said, standing up and gesticulating widely. "Mere puppets . . . mere things . . . pushed and pulled, and told and directed. But will they listen to our suggestions? Do we have any influence at all? NO! O-o-o-oh, I would like, just once, to be able to tell them what to do to fix up this world."

"I suppose," Oggy laughed, "that you'd know just what to do!"

"Of course," said Arabella.

4

Stirring Up a Breeze

The next day was even hotter, and though the tree house was possibly the coolest place in town, there was no denying *it was hot*. Arabella sat cross-legged, alternating between working on a crossword puzzle and using it to fan herself.

"Well," Melinda said, stretching, "even if it is hot, I had better do some dusting for you, Oggy. ZoZo Sejura will be here in just two days."

"How come all this fuss about ZoZo Sejura?" asked Murk. "What is actually so grand about him?"

"My father says he is a very charming boy," said Melinda. "But besides that, the Sejuras are *terribly* important. We have to make them see that Americans are very nice."

"Some Americans are," said Arabella, shrugging, "and some aren't."

"Well, *we* are," said Melinda.

"I suppose we are," said Arabella.

"But why all the razzle-dazzle?" asked Murk. "They'll probably like us fine. What's the worry?"

"I don't know," said Melinda. "Not exactly. It has something to do with diplomacy."

"What it is, no doubt," said Arabella, now using the puzzle for a fan, "is that world problems have made it advisable for our country to be especially nice to the small countries that we have always sort of taken for granted. We need them, you see, so they will be on our side in world conflicts. That's strange," she said, going back to her puzzle, "I thought I knew all the possible synonyms for encomium, but none seems to fit. Mmmmm, let's see. Ha! panegyric, but that's inexact, really. Very poor puzzle!"

"Arabella!" said Oggy. "Sometimes you make me sick!" He played an uncomplimentary razz on the oboe.

"Oggy," reproached Melinda, "Arabella can't help it if she's smart."

Murk was examining the construction of the tree

house. It was very good work and really quite clever, because, as a matter of fact, the tree house was not strictly in a tree. "Hey," said Murk, "this tree house is really more of a stump house, isn't it?" Oggy bristled.

But, of course, there had been a tree, a marvelous maple, dear to the hearts of the Clay family, but lightning had struck it some years before. When the tree surgeons were done with it, there was not much left but the lower part of the huge trunk and two strong main branches that rose from the trunk in a wide "Y." "Oh, it looks awful," Mrs. Clay had said. "Heartbreaking!" Mr. Clay felt bad too, until it occurred to him that the "Y" was the perfect foundation for a tree house—the kind he had always wanted when he was a boy. Mrs. Clay approved. It would be a good way to keep Oggy busy at home. Mr. Clay built it sturdy as a ship—the kind he had helped build for the Navy. The platform was of seasoned planks, set close and varnished. The house itself, though rustic in appearance, was very sturdy and comfortably furnished with canvas cots, air mattresses, neat shelves, a cupboard, a built-in table, and a water cooler, which Oggy kept filled with fresh water. There were blinds on the windows, and as a fine architectural touch, Mr.

Clay had built a chimney on the house. It was just for *looks*, he had said. As it turned out, he was wrong.

Murk finished his inspection by examining the platform railing, which was actually from an old ship, very strong and handsome. Then he threw himself down on the bench, which was at one end of the platform, and stared up at the trees surrounding the tree house. The leaves seemed not to move at all, except when a caterpillar stirred or a bird alighted for a moment.

Arabella followed his gaze. "Not a breeze. Not a bit of one," she said. "This is the stillest day I ever heard." Oggy started to play his oboe softly. "It's strange when nothing moves at all," Arabella went on, "as though everything were baked solid just the way it is. I wish we had a fan to stir things up a little."

Melinda, who was just finishing her dusting, said, "Oh, a fan would be marvelous."

"Don't be silly," said Murk, "you couldn't plug it in here. There's no power. Unless, of course, you had a generator. Hey! You want me to bring you my generator, Oggy?"

"I don't know," said Oggy. "Do I?"

"What, exactly, is a generator?" asked Arabella.

"Gee," said Murk, not unhappily, "for a bright kid sometimes you're *not* too smart."

"Never mind that," said Arabella. "One of the attributes of true intellect is the willingness to acknowledge gaps in one's knowledge. I just don't happen to have got around to the study of mechanics as yet. I'm not really ready to concern myself with it too much even now, so just be brief, please."

"Okay," said Murk cheerfully. "A generator is a machine that can make electricity itself, by burning some kind of fuel, see."

"Like gasoline?" asked Oggy.

"Yes, like gasoline."

"I never saw one," said Oggy.

"Well," said Murk, "if you want to come on down to my shed with me, we could carry it up here. It's not heavy. Then we could try attaching a fan to it."

"That would be wonderful," said Arabella. "While you're getting the generator, I'll go get the fan from my bedroom."

An hour later the generator, about the size of a large radio, was clacketing away on the platform of the tree house and Murk was regarding it with satisfaction. "That's a really fine little generator," he said. "Listen to it. Smooth and regular, and good and strong. Okay, let's try the fan." Oggy switched on the fan, and Melinda's long chestnut hair blew across her face.

"Oh, it's lovely," she said, standing closer.

"It *is* lovely," said Arabella. "The only trouble is that the fan only seems big enough to cool one person at a time—the one who stands right in front of it. Come on, Melinda, give me a chance now."

Murk said, "Yes, we really need a bigger fan. Much bigger." His mind was now churning around on his favorite subject. "Much, much bigger! Hey! I just thought of something. In my shed there's all this stuff of my grandfather's, you know."

"We know," said Oggy, with a touch of disgust. "Wow, what junk!"

"Well, some of isn't so good," agreed Murk. "But junk is pretty valuable sometimes. Anyhow, there's this big old fan sort of thing that my grandfather made for a propeller for a kind of aircraft he was inventing."

"But it didn't work," said Oggy.

"No," said Murk, "it didn't work. But it might

work as a big sort of ceiling fan, see. It's on a thick metal pole, and we could mount it on the roof of the tree house . . . if you don't mind," he said to Oggy.

"Could it come off whenever we don't want it anymore?" asked Oggy. "I don't want to do anything to spoil the looks of the house, you know."

"Sure," said Murk. "Just leave it to me. But you can come help me carry it. It's pretty heavy, and we'll need to bring some tools and things, too."

It was quite a feat of engineering just to get the enormous fan up the rope ladder, but it was done. The children stood regarding it. "It's awfully big," said Melinda.

"What's this for?" asked Arabella, pointing to a lever on the metal pole that held the fan.

Murk moved the lever with some difficulty, since it was a bit out of the habit of moving. "Look," he said, "it moves the blades of the fan to change the angle. See, my grandfather had this on the back of his airplane. He thought it would drive the plane forward, and that he could make it go up or down by changing the pitch of these blades. The only trouble was that the plane didn't fly."

"Why not?" asked Arabella.

"He wasn't sure," said Murk. "It flew on paper. Now listen, Oggy, could we let this pole go down through the chimney and just bolt it to the floor of the tree house? It would be steadiest that way."

"Okay," said Oggy. "Just as long as you don't hurt anything."

"Won't make a scratch," said Murk, and together they lifted the fan, which looked like a small windmill. When Murk had it neatly rigged, it gave a new height and importance to the house.

"Hey!" said Oggy. "That chimney has some use after all. That looks pretty good!" Murk was pleased.

"Well, let's try it," said Arabella impatiently.

"Okay," said Murk. "Now, when we want to turn it on, we just switch this button, see," and he switched it.

The big fan started up, at first slowly, with a wide swooping *swish*. Melinda's hair swept back in the downdraft, and Arabella threw her head back and got the cool wind on her neck.

"Wow!" exclaimed Oggy. "Is that cool!"

"*That's* what I call a fan!" said Murk, and as he said it, the fan's great blades whirled faster, and all at once the tree house began to quiver and shake and tremble, and Oggy cried, "Hey, look! Over in the corner! The platform's starting to tip! Turn it off! Turn it off!"

Murk leaped for the switch.

When the big fan had stopped whizzing, Murk said, "Well, it *may* be a bit *too* big. That's a shame."

"Oh, that was so nice and cool, too," said Melinda.

"Gee, that's some fan your grandfather built!" Oggy said. "It might not have been much of a propeller, but it is a great old fan."

"Yeah," said Murk. "And that was only low speed. Well! I'm sorry. Maybe we can hook up a couple of more little fans."

"Anyhow," said Arabella, "it was a delightful half-minute."

5

Trouble for Miss Shrubb

The town of Goodbury, in the county of Meredith, was neat and tidy in the center of town, rolling and green as it crossed the river and got out to the country, but ragged around the edges as it reached the town limits, finally becoming downright shaggy at the town dump and junkyard. But just beyond the junkyard, on the other side of the road, was a large and marvelous tidal marsh, thick with reeds and grasses, alive with wonderful wild creatures, and overlooked by almost everyone in Meredith County except a few duck hunters and a certain Miss Shrubb.

Miss Shrubb was a tiny person, with very little more bulk than a shard of marsh grass, but just as wiry and just as suited to life in the marsh. Because, as it happened, there at the very edge of the marsh, on a little piece of solid dry meadow, Miss Shrubb lived surrounded by wild ducks and geese, gulls and terns, coots and rails, herons, egrets and grebes—not to mention loons. She lived in a small cottage constructed of two large packing cases, and a most tidy and adequate home she had made. It was while acquiring an occasional furnishing for her cottage that she had come to know Murk Kitt, and together they would forage in the discarded junk of Meredith County. Sometimes Murk would find something that Miss Shrubb could use—an excellent chair with only one leg missing, a pot or pan. And Miss Shrubb, for her part, always was alert for the sight of some useful tool or bolt for Murk.

Sometimes Miss Shrubb would pause in her work to watch a bird in flight, and many times she had pointed out to Murk an unusual bird stopping in the protective marsh during its long migratory flight.

Miss Shrubb's resemblance to a bird was marked, and her diet was quite similar. She lived largely on the things the marsh provided—wild asparagus, currants, blueberries, raspberries, some shellfish, and an occasional duck egg. In the little garden surrounding

her cottage, she grew carrots, parsley, and potatoes,
though, she told Murk, it was a struggle, since these
plants really preferred somewhat drier surroundings.

In the winter, when the garden was bare and the
marsh provided little to eat, Miss Shrubb went into
business, in a small way. She would weave little baskets
of marsh grasses, brightly color them with berry dyes,
and sell them to the people of Goodbury and the surrounding towns. The ladies of Meredith County all

had sewing baskets, bread baskets, shopping baskets, and trinket baskets woven by Miss Shrubb and sold for pennies, which she immediately spent at the grocery store for her winter supplies. While she was looked upon as odd and perhaps not quite . . . well, acceptable, she was so quiet and pleasant that the people of Meredith County, for the most part, tolerated Miss Shrubb or overlooked her completely.

Overlooked her, that is, until a certain day in July. It was the day before the arrival of ZoZo Sejura and his father, the Ambassador from Peroque, *and two days before what happened happened.*

On that certain day in July, Mayor Kronk of Goodbury announced a decision which he thought a wise one for an election year. He called his advisors together to tell them about it. "In an election year," he said, "the best thing for an administration to do is to do something popular." The advisors nodded their heads. "I've been thinking it over," said Mayor Kronk, "and I have been thinking that the thing that would be most popular in Goodbury is a good racetrack."

"A racetrack!" exclaimed one of the advisors in spite of himself.

"Yes, a racetrack!" said the Mayor. "Anything wrong with that?"

"No, sir, it's just, well . . . people gamble at racetracks, you know."

"Of course, I know," said the Mayor. "That's the idea. People like to gamble. It's popular. And I just finished telling you, I want to do something popular. Now, there's a fellow in the city interested in leasing land and building us a racetrack, and all in all, it's a dandy idea. Right?"

"Right," the advisors said weakly.

"But . . ." started one advisor, but he thought better of it and stopped.

"Yes, but . . . ?" asked the Mayor.

"Well," said the advisor. "There's not a place in town that's flat enough for a racetrack."

But Mayor Kronk had the answer to that. "We're going to fill in the marsh in back of the junkyard," he said. "Nothing to it. First we push all that stuff on the dump into the marsh, then we keep dumping in the marsh for a little while, and before you know it we have a nice big hunk of flat land for the racetrack."

"Well, you know," said one of the advisors, "there's a person actually living on the marsh."

"Miss Slug," said the Mayor.

"Shrubb," said the advisor.

"Doesn't matter," said the Mayor. "She's a squatter. Illegal in the first place. We'll shoo her off. Right away."

"But suppose she doesn't want to go?" asked the advisor.

"No problem," said the Mayor. "I'll send the marshals down there with a bill for back rent she owes the town, and an order to send her to the poor farm if she can't pay. Easy. I'll do it first thing in the morning and clear the way for progress."

The advisors had to admit that the Mayor had it all worked out.

6

Arabella Decides

It was Murk who brought the bad news to the tree house. He was quite upset. "She told me herself," he said. "The town marshals came down and said she had to move out of the marsh."

"And what did she say?" asked Arabella.

"She said she didn't want to. But they said, okay, then they would be down later with an order for her to pay back rent to the town, and if she couldn't pay it, they would take her to the poor farm."

"Wow!" said Oggy.

Arabella looked furious. "Oooooo!" she shouted. And she stamped.

"And the thing is," said Murk, "she is upset because what they're going to do is fill in the marsh."

"Fill it in!" exclaimed Arabella. "That's awful!"

"But why?" asked Oggy. "What's awful?"

"Miss Shrubb says that if they fill in that marsh it is a little bit of the end of the world," said Murk.

"What does she mean?" asked Oggy. "It sure sounds scary. I mean . . ." and he looked sideways at Arabella, but she didn't seem to notice his admission.

"Well, she's romanticizing," said Arabella, "but I know what she means. It's the balance of nature—when you spoil any part of it, it upsets all the other parts because everything in nature depends on everything else. Especially in a tidal marsh like that."

"I guess sometimes all that stuff you know about comes in handy," said Oggy in a tone as regretful as it was admiring.

"Sometimes," said Arabella. "Oh, poor Miss Shrubb!"

"I just don't know how she will live away from the marsh," said Murk. "It's her home."

"Oh, it's so highhanded," said Arabella. "It's the sort of thing to make your blood boil."

"How will she make her baskets if she doesn't live in the marsh?" asked Oggy. "She won't have any way of making a living."

"When they told her she could go to the poor farm," said Murk, "she said she hadn't realized, till then, that she was poor. And honestly, she isn't! It's just she doesn't have stuff, you know."

Arabella was pacing around the tree-house platform, her forehead drawn into deep creases, her mouth puckered. Suddenly she stamped her foot. "No!" she shouted. "No! It's another example of fuzzy adult thinking. It smacks of the kind of highhanded injustice that, however legal, can never be right. It tastes of feudalism and the reign of tyrants. No! We shall not sit idly by. We *must* act!" Her voice was quavering when she said, "Bring her here, Murk!"

"Here?" asked Murk.

"Here?" asked Oggy. "Hey! *Here?*"

"Oggy," said Arabella, "everything has a purpose, and what could possibly be the purpose of a tree house?"

"To play in," said Oggy promptly. "That's what it's for."

"That's what it *seems* to be for," said Arabella, "but true purpose is not always apparent. Anything as fine as this may have a more significant function—to shelter a homeless lady, for example. To aid in the cause of justice."

"I'd better ask my ma," said Oggy.

"Oggy," said Arabella, holding up a warning hand, "would that be productive?"

"No," said Oggy. "I guess not." But he still looked very doubtful. Arabella went on, undeterred by his doubts.

"Murk," she said, pointing in the direction of the marsh, "go and bring her here before the marshals come back. Quickly!"

"How do you know she'll come with me?"

"Try it," said Arabella. "Tell her we want to help her. Go ahead. And don't let anyone see you." And then Arabella sat down and hugged her trembling knees.

"You can't be cold," said Oggy.

"No," whispered Arabella. "No, I'm not cold."

An hour later, through fields and back alleys, Murk and Miss Shrubb were traversing the eastern quadrant of the town of Goodbury—he, stocky but swift and agile; she, a small brown leaf blowing along beside him, carrying all her possessions in a reed basket and scattering crumbs to the birds as she came.

In the meanwhile, Arabella had not been idle. She had ransacked the Serafin kitchen and had packed

some paper bags with cans of soups and fruit, a cheese, and a loaf of bread. Oggy had brought in an extra blanket, in case the night was chill, filled the water cooler, and otherwise checked the housekeeping facilities of the tree house. His enthusiasm grew as he worked because he was very proud of his shipshape abode.

When Murk and Miss Shrubb arrived in the Clay yard, it was late afternoon and the long shadows of the birches and beeches were a protective veil over the garden. Murk helped the tiny and only slightly confused Miss Shrubb up the rope ladder, and when she stood on the platform, swathed in her long brown skirts and several sweaters, she was puffing warmly because, at the moment, she was wearing nearly every piece of clothing she owned. She took off two of her sweaters before she said a thing.

"How very nice of you!" she said then. "How very nice of you to ask me." She looked around. "How lovely! How charming!" Then she looked up at the leaves of the nearby trees, which were like a garden in the sky. "How beautiful!" And then she threw the last of her few bread crumbs to two passing sparrows.

Arabella stepped forward and held out her hand. "I'm Arabella Serafin," she said, "and this is Oggy Clay. This is his tree house."

"How do you do, Arabella," said Miss Shrubb, taking Arabella's hand in her tiny one. Then she turned to Oggy. "Thank you very much for your kind hospitality, Oggy."

Oggy gave a small bow which he thought was suitable for a host.

Then Miss Shrubb stepped out of two of her skirts,

whereupon, as if by magic, she immediately became even smaller.

"Miss Shrubb," said Arabella, "we want to help you, but at the moment we are not sure just how. We are not very influential, you know, because, unfortunately, technically we are children."

"Ah, well," said Miss Shrubb, "don't feel too badly about that. Technically, I am adult, and I have not a mite of influence."

"Well, anyway," said Oggy, "at least we can hide you here until we can think of what to do."

"We are going to have to think of some way to make those adults see some reason," said Arabella. "Maybe all of us thinking together may help."

Murk looked around. "Hey! Where's Melinda been all day? In all the excitement I forgot about her."

"Her Very Important Visitor, ZoZo Sejura, arrived today," said Oggy, "and she went to the airport with her family to meet him."

A call was heard from across the garden. "Arabella!" Mrs. Serafin was summoning her daughter.

"Oop!" said Arabella, jumping to her feet, "I'd better get home quickly before my mother comes looking for me. I'll be up to see you first thing in the morning, Miss Shrubb. Just stay hidden in the tree house. No grown-ups ever come up here. I hope you won't be lonely."

"Good-bye, and thank you," said Miss Shrubb. "I shall be fine. I am quite used to being by myself, and I have a great deal to think about—I shall be mourning my beautiful marsh and all the wild things." And her sweet face became so sad that even the sensible Arabella felt quite moved.

Then Oggy and Murk said good night and promised to come in the morning. Night fell on the tree house.

7

A Very Important Visitor

Arabella was the first to arrive at the tree house the next morning. She found Miss Shrubb smiling brightly and sharing her breakfast with some neighborhood sparrows.

"Good morning. Good morning," chirped Miss Shrubb.

"Did you sleep well?" inquired Arabella.

"Quite perfectly," said Miss Shrubb. "I am not used to such comforts. Dear me, you may spoil me."

Arabella put away a few things she had brought with her—a package of cornflakes, some oranges, and a jar of peach preserve. Then Oggy arrived with fresh water for the cooler, a bag of bananas, and his oboe.

"I had quite forgotten," said Miss Shrubb, as she

swept the platform of the tree house, "how pleasant it is to have company. So few people come to see me at the cottage in the marsh. Murk is just about my only caller."

"Why do you like the marsh so much, Miss Shrubb?" asked Arabella. "It seems an awfully wet place to live, if you'll forgive my saying so."

"Well, it is wet," agreed Miss Shrubb, "but few places are entirely perfect. Some, for instance, are too dry. And the marsh feels right to me. I am at home. I feel I am walking about where life begins. I love the wild things of the marsh, and I do truly believe," she said shyly, "that they care for me and trust me. How often the ducks and I have hidden together in the tall grasses, while the hunters tried to lure us from the marsh. But we are too clever for them. And then we learn from each other, the creatures and I." Her face clouded. "Now what will become of them, when they fill the marshland? Where will the ducks hide? Where will the geese feed? Where will the herons nest? And my timid bitterns?"

Arabella studied Miss Shrubb's troubled face. "Oh!" she said with exasperation. "We have just got to make them listen to us!"

Just then, Melinda's light voice was heard from the ground. "Hallooo, up there," she called. "I've brought a Very Important Visitor to see you. May we come up, Oggy?"

Oggy came to the edge of the platform and looked over. There was Melinda dressed in the freshest, newest, pinkest dress anyone had ever seen, and beside her, in a sparkling white suit, was a small boy with very dark bright eyes that seemed so enormous there was just room on his face to squeeze in a tiny nose and mouth. He was smiling with anticipation.

"Come on up," said Oggy, the host, as the others came to the edge of the platform to greet the visitor.

Melinda said, "This is ZoZo Sejura, everyone." And then she said, "ZoZo, this is Oggy, and this is Arabella, and . . ." and then she saw Miss Shrubb and hesitated.

Arabella said, "Melinda, you know Miss Shrubb . . . from the marsh. She's staying here for a while." Melinda took the opportunity to bob one of her curtsies, and Miss Shrubb smiled at her and at ZoZo.

"Well, then," said Melinda, drawing a sigh of relief, "that's everyone introduced. Do you like it?" She waved at the tree house.

"I like!" exclaimed ZoZo, smiling broadly. "I

would like for me, myself. When I go home I ask my papa for a tree house for me."

Oggy took ZoZo in hand then and started to give him the grand guided tour, pointing out the comfortable cots and air mattresses and the now well-stocked cupboards.

"And what this is?" asked ZoZo, pointing to the little fan in the corner of the platform. Oggy switched it on to show him. The fan started to whirr up a comfortable breeze, although it was hardly necessary at that hour of the morning.

"And what this is?" asked ZoZo, pointing to the other switch.

"Oh, that's for the big top fan," said Oggy, "but it seems to have some bugs in it."

"What this bugs is?" ZoZo asked, just as a commotion from under the tree house caused their attention to turn to the rope ladder.

The commotion was caused by Murk, who was talking fast, breathing hard, and climbing the rope ladder as if pursued. It turned out that he was.

"It's the marshals!" he panted as he reached the top of the ladder. "They're after me!"

"After *you?*" fretted Miss Shrubb. "I should think they would be after *me!*"

"They are," said Murk, still out of breath. "You see, I was down at the junkyard scouting around, and then I thought I'd stop by your cottage and see if there was anything else you might need. And then the marshals showed up. They started asking me questions—did I know where you were—and, well I tried to lie, but I'm not good at it. I guess they figured I knew something. Anyhow, I decided to beat it, and I got a good start on them. They followed me, but I know some back alleys and I lost them. For now."

"Ooooo!" said Arabella. "But they only have to go to your house and your mother will say you might be here, and then they'll find you, and Miss Shrubb, too."

"Yes," said Murk miserably. "I know."

"What *is* this all about?" asked Melinda.

"It's Miss Shrubb," said Arabella in a hurry. "They're going to send her to the poor farm for not paying rent to the town. It's just to bully her and harass her. *Now* what are we going to do?"

And as Arabella said "do," there was a sudden whirring sound that nobody immediately identified, a strong breeze started to blow, and the tree house began to shudder and shake. Melinda clutched Miss Shrubb to steady herself, Arabella sat down suddenly, and

Murk grabbed the railing and looked about confusedly. It was when he saw the wide-eyed ZoZo standing beside the generator that he knew what had happened. The big fan on top of the tree house was spinning so fast you could see only a blur. Murk yelled, "Hey! Did you turn the switch? Hey! Turn it off!" And he started to crawl across the heaving platform to the generator. Then suddenly, with a loud ripping sound, the tree house was lifted from its perch on the tree stump and within a second was flying quite free. Airborne!

"Hey! You deedn't tell me the house fly!" cried ZoZo delightedly.

"Turn it off!" screamed Oggy, who was clinging to the big bench. "Hey, Murk! Turn it off!"

"It's too late now," said Murk with wonder in his voice. "If I turn it off now we'll just crash to the ground."

Melinda was crying. Miss Shrubb was her quiet self, accepting this as just one of the things that happen.

Arabella was recovering her senses. "Murk!" she exclaimed. "This may not be altogether bad, you know. Can you steer it or anything?"

Murk considered the matter. He looked down. The

tree house was hovering just about at the tops of the trees. "Well," he said, "we can try."

While the children held their breath and watched, Murk went over to the metal pole that supported the big whirring fan and gave a tentative push to the lever that controlled the angle of the blades. Because they were spinning so fast, it was impossible to see the direct effect on them, but there was an immediate effect on the tree house. It started to move forward . . . ever so slowly . . . but forward, toward the birches that separated the Clay garden from the Serafin garden.

"You did it, Murk!" said Arabella. "What else can you do?"

"I don't know," said Murk, scarcely believing his luck. "But I'll see." Slowly he dipped the blades in the other direction; the tree house began to back up.

"Hey!" cried Oggy. "You can really drive it."

"What if you want to turn to the right," asked Arabella, "and go off over the field?"

Murk thought about it. "I don't see what I can do to the blades to make them do that. If I tip them more in one direction, I think we should head downward, and in the other we would head upward; but what could I do to make them turn right or left? Wait a minute." He went to the back of the platform and

looked at the little fan that Oggy had switched on a while before. "Have you got any rope, Oggy?"

Oggy looked around. "The only rope is the cord of the venetian blinds in the house."

"Okay, that'll do," said Murk. "We can tie this fan onto the back railing, then I can try tipping it around. It just might act like a kind of rudder." And that is just exactly what it did. When Murk had rigged it up, he tried tilting the fan first to the right, then to the left. "Hey, it works!" he cried. "Look at this," and he tipped the fan carefully. The tree house made a gentle turn to the right and started to move slowly but steadily out toward the meadow.

"Stay out of sight of our kitchen window," cautioned Arabella. "My mother may be back from the market by now. I'd rather not have her see this just yet." Murk turned the rudder fan a bit more, and the tree house responded beautifully.

Miss Shrubb said, "Well, I never!" Melinda, who had been clinging to her the whole time, started to relax. "It's nice," she said.

Oggy went over to the saucer-eyed ZoZo. "Boy! What you did!" he said.

"I?" asked ZoZo. "I made house fly?"

"You sure did," said Murk, not in the least displeased, as he experimented a bit more with the rudder fan, perfecting his skill. "Look," he said, "I think I can make it go a little faster by switching the top fan onto high speed." He tried it, and the tree house picked up speed. "Oh boy!" exclaimed Murk with satisfaction. "My grandfather should have seen this!"

8

This Is Where We Came In

The tree house continued across the meadow, crossed the river, flew over the little woods, cleared the tree-tops nicely, skirted the junkyard, and flew over the marsh.

"Oh, my!" breathed Miss Shrubb. "What a treat! Look at that lovely marsh. This is just the way the birds see it as they fly over."

Murk turned the rudder fan a bit, and they veered inland over the treetops and out into the open country. There was no one about, and except for an occasional car on the road, there was no sign of life.

"I guess everyone must be at market on a Saturday morning," said Arabella.

"Listen!" Oggy said suddenly. "Couldn't we *do* something?"

"For heaven's sake," said Arabella, "we *are* doing something!"

But Murk said, "Do what?"

"Anything!" cried Oggy, throwing his arms wide. "Anything at all! Let's . . . let's bomb the school!"

"Oh, Oggy, you're silly!" said Arabella.

"Oh, I don't really mean bomb it," said Oggy. "I mean do *something* to it."

Murk said, "We *could* bomb it."

"Oh, boy, bomb!" cried ZoZo.

"No!" cried Melinda and Miss Shrubb.

Arabella said scornfully, "Don't worry."

And yet, when Murk had steered the tree house into a strategic position over the empty schoolhouse, neither Melinda nor Arabella could long resist joining in the bombardment. Oggy filled the paper grocery bags with water from the cooler and these were dropped with precision on the classrooms.

"Gotcha!" cried Oggy as he bombed Miss Prilly's room. "Gotcha!"

The janitor came out and squinted up at the sun. "Rainin'!" he muttered, and went back inside.

"Save one for Miss Rudolph's room," begged Melinda. "Just one." But the bags were exhausted too soon.

"If I'd only known," mourned Arabella, "I would have taken more bags from the kitchen."

"We could shoot the place with a blowgun or something," said Oggy.

"Nah!" Murk said. "We bombed it. It's demolished."

"Well then, let's just *go* somewhere," said Oggy, gesturing extravagantly.

Murk turned the tree house toward the outskirts of town again. They flew over the little woods once more and then out into the open country.

"Look at the cows," said Melinda. "They look like they have no legs when you see them from above."

Then they were flying over an enormous cornfield . . . the cornfield of Mr. Samuel Manoover. And *that* is when Mr. Manoover first thought he saw them and went into the farmhouse to tell Mrs. Manoover. And *that* is when Mrs. Manoover said, "Shame on you, Sam Manoover!"

Arabella was the first to notice a clear strip of uncultivated land running in between two fields of corn. "Look," she said. "Sometime we are going to want to come down, and I was just thinking it might be hard to do."

"I've been thinking about that myself," confessed Murk.

"Well, so now what I'm thinking—among many other things that I am thinking—is that a clear piece of field like that might be a good place."

"Oh, don't come down, please," cried ZoZo. "I like up here. Why you not tell me house can fly?" he reproached Melinda.

"Well, we all like it up here," said Murk, "but the fact is sometime we are going to need to come down because of gasoline, for one thing. And sometime we are going to have to come down, anyway. And I have been thinking, too, that when we do come down, we are going to get hollered at."

"Putting it mildly," agreed Arabella. Melinda began to cry. They circled the cornfield several times, Murk steering the tree house so that they got a good view of the farm, the barn, the well, and the vegetable gardens. "Listen," said Arabella, "I won't trouble you with my step-by-step reasoning, but I have come to certain conclusions."

"What kind of conclusions?" asked Oggy.

"Well, obviously this is an unusually fine flying craft, quite capable of keeping us aloft and comfortable for as yet undetermined lengths of time."

"Yes," said Murk, "one of the first things we have got to find out is *what* length of time, or we are going to have quite a bump." Melinda, who had stopped crying to listen to Arabella, began to cry again. Miss Shrubb comforted her.

"Now," said Arabella, "as Murk pointed out, we may be in for strong disciplinary action. No one is going to believe this was an accident."

Oggy said quickly, "I know it! They'll think we did it on purpose, and we're going to get punished, for sure. Especially me."

"Now," Arabella continued, "the other important thing to consider is our obligation to Miss Shrubb. We have undertaken to hide her. If we go home now we are going to give her away . . . right into the hands of the law. I think we just have to consider staying out of reach until we can think of a way of making this turn out better."

"How do you think we can do that?" sobbed Melinda.

"I don't know yet," said Arabella, "but we can get to work on it right away. Meanwhile, I think we ought to fly back to town and just let our parents know we are all right. That's the only decent thing to do. We don't want them to worry."

"Ah, that's very thoughtful, Arabella," said Miss Shrubb, as Murk steered the tree house out over the orchard and down the road to town. It was amusing, as they flew low over the town park, to see the children playing below on the playground.

"It's like looking down on ourselves," said Arabella. And *that* is when one of the children on the swings was attracted to the noise overhead and saw them. They watched as he ran to tell his mother, but she seemed to pay no attention.

"Just as well," said Arabella. "People are bound to see us sooner or later, but for the moment I think we are better off unnoticed."

Then they flew over the Serafin yard, and *that* is when Mr. and Mrs. Serafin came running to see what was happening. And *that* is what was happening.

"Wow!" said Murk as he flew the tree house across the meadow and toward the woods, "I'm glad it was *your* mother and father and not mine. I don't think my father would have taken 'no' for an answer."

"Usually, my father wouldn't either," said Arabella, a strange light coming into her eyes. "But I am beginning to think we may be in a rather unusual position." She looked thoughtful.

"Well, anyway, let's head for that cornfield and see if we can make a landing."

Murk was becoming expert at steering, and Oggy, feeling relieved at postponing discipline, asked for a chance at the tiller. Murk generously let him steer, with ZoZo helping, while he went around and checked the performance of the generator and the main fan. "Fine craft!" he said with satisfaction. "Couldn't have designed a better one."

As they came over the cornfields, Murk took the controls again and started giving orders. "Oggy," he said, "switch the top fan to low speed." Oggy did it and the tree house slowed. "Now tilt the blades of the fan to the down position," ordered Murk. Oggy tilted, but the tree house slowly started to climb. "No, no!" said Murk. "The other way!" And when Oggy had complied, the tree house slowly started down . . . down, down, slowly down, until it gently touched the clearing in the cornfield.

"Okay, off with the switch!" cried Murk, and the big fan whirred to a stop.

"Wow! Perfect landing!" cried Oggy, and he leaped over the railing of the tree house and onto the green grass of the clearing.

"Look," said Melinda, "it's just like being in a jungle. Those cornstalks are so high they're almost like trees."

"That's the idea," said Arabella. "We can't be seen from the road or any of the houses around. Perhaps we will be able to stay here, hide Miss Shrubb, make our plans, and spend the night."

"Oh!" cried ZoZo, delighted. "You not tell me we make camp, yes?"

"Oh, ZoZo," cried Melinda, "I didn't *know* it."

"Ah! Surprise, yes?" said ZoZo.

9

A Secret Society

And just then Mr. Manoover, who had been having a morning nap in the cornstalks, arose and squinted. "There it is again," he said to himself, "and it does look real." He walked out and hailed the children a bit hesitantly. "Hey!" he called.

The children were startled. "Quickly!" cried Melinda. "Murk, start it up again! He'll tell on us."

"Hush," said Arabella. "Let me handle this." She approached Mr. Manoover. When she had nearly reached him, she did an astonishing thing. She stood on one foot, turned on her heel, bent one leg, pushed the other straight out in front of her, and shot both her arms up into the air. Then she stood up.

"Hey! What's that?" asked Mr. Manoover.

"That's the formal greeting to a stranger in our secret society," said Arabella.

"Y'don't say!" said Mr. Manoover, impressed. "And what society is that, if I may ask?"

"Fly-In," Arabella improvised.

"Y'don't say!" cried Mr. Manoover. "Oooooh, I've got a good mind not to tell Mrs. Manoover about this. She'd say I was imagining it. Why, she didn't even believe it this morning when I told her I saw this . . . this *thing* flying over the orchard."

"You saw us this morning?" asked Oggy, getting brave and coming forward.

"Salute the stranger," said Arabella, and Oggy stared at her for a moment.

"Ahhhh . . . Arabella," he protested.

"Oggy!" said Arabella. And so Oggy got down on one leg, as Arabella had done, shot the other out in front of him, and went through the whole complicated display.

"Very nice," said Mr. Manoover. "Real courteous. Showy."

"You say your wife didn't believe you when you said you had seen us flying around?" asked Arabella. "Why?"

"That woman!" Mr. Manoover said with exasperation. "That woman, good cook though she be, she has not believed a thing I have told her in the last dozen years."

"Why is that?" asked Miss Shrubb with kindly interest. "Do you . . . do you . . . ?"

"Exaggerate?" Melinda filled in.

"Lor', no!" said Mr. Manoover. "But I lie. Got the habit some time back." He chuckled. "No harm intended ever, of course."

"Well," said Arabella, "if she won't believe you, in

any case, why not just keep it a secret—our being in your field?" She became quite confidential. "We might even be able to make you a member of our secret society."

"Oh, lor'!" said Mr. Manoover. "That idea does really delight me. I never did belong to nothing, not at all. There they are"—he waved at the world at large—"knowing stuff I don't know . . . not believing me. But they don't even know who grows the corn they eat . . . they don't. Well! *Now* we'll see who has a secret. Eh! Well! Care for some medicinal spirits?" He shoved his bottle toward Miss Shrubb, politely, since she was the eldest guest.

Miss Shrubb took it and sniffed it. "Oh, dear, no," she said. "It seems too . . . er . . . robust a drink for us."

Mr. Manoover took it back and sniffed it, too. "I believe you may be right," he said.

"Now," said Arabella thoughtfully, when they had all settled themselves and were eating a late lunch of bread, jam, and canned peaches, in a friendly circle on the grass, "for a secret society to exist, it has to be *kept* a secret."

"Cor-rect!" said Mr. Manoover. "I agree to that."

"Good," said Arabella, "because, after all, you will be the member most important to the keeping of our secret."

"Me!" exclaimed Mr. Manoover, beaming with pride. "Gosh!"

"Do you think we could stay here in your cornfield for a while?"

"Welcome!" said Mr. Manoover.

"We may need to borrow a few things." Arabella was serious and businesslike.

"Like some gasoline . . ." said Murk.

"Oh, I have some gasoline," said Mr. Manoover. "I have gasoline to run the tractor. And you can make yourselves at home. Use the well . . . anytime you like. And help yerself to the vegetable garden . . . only stay out of sight of the house."

"How about anyone else?" asked Arabella. "Is there anyone else on the farm?"

"Not now," said Mr. Manoover. "Come harvest, I'll have me some help. But now there's just me and Missus."

"All right," said Arabella, "then we won't waste time discussing the mechanics and logistics. I think they will all work out quite simply." Arabella became quite relaxed and cheerful.

"What about sleeping?" asked Melinda. "How are we all going to sleep? There are only two beds."

Oggy had an idea about that. "There are two air mattresses," he said. "They're fine by themselves just on the ground. And the two cots are made of canvas and are fine by themselves. So that's four beds."

"But there are six of us," said Melinda.

"How about a bed of nice fresh straw," suggested Mr. Manoover. "I've got plenty of straw."

"Oh, lovely," said Miss Shrubb. "I adore the smell of clean straw. I should like that myself. We can use my extra skirts for blankets."

"That'll be fine for me, too," said Murk.

"So let's consider the important details of this situation," said Arabella. "What are they?"

"In the first place," said Murk, "by now everybody's going to be looking for us."

"Well, they'll have a hard time finding us here," said Oggy.

"We'll have to be careful coming and going," said Murk. "And keep our landing field a secret."

"We could camouflage the tree house with cornstalks," suggested Oggy.

Mr. Manoover grinned, contemplating his field as part of the secret. "Good field," he said. "Grew some fine corn here last year. Field's resting this year, you know. Next year, plant it again, you know. Next year, rest another field, see. Get mighty fine corn that way."

"Okay," said Arabella. "We can stay hidden on the ground and out of reach up in the air. Two safe places. Oh, think of it!" She grinned. "Out of reach of grown-ups for the first time in our lives—and blamelessly, you might say, through no fault of our own . . ."

"Arabella," said Miss Shrubb reproachfully, "you *are* rationalizing a bit."

Arabella considered. "All right," she agreed, "that's true. We are not blameless, because we *are* willfully remaining out of reach. But the thing is, we just can't let this situation go by without examining its possibilities."

"What possibilities?" asked Murk.

"They remain to be seen," said Arabella.

10

The Second Flight

The rest of the afternoon was quite relaxing and delightful, and entirely different from the first few weeks of summer. Arabella wandered down to the brook with Miss Shrubb, and they sat on a rock and cooled their bare feet in the water. ZoZo found Mr. Manoover's old, nearly white horse in the lower pasture, and from that moment they were quite inseparable. Melinda tidied up the tree house and set the table for supper. Oggy and Murk went to the barn with Mr. Manoover and got a can of gasoline, a few tools, and a handy coil of rope. When they came back from the barn they also carried a gallon of milk, which Mr. Manoover said the cow was happy to send. Murk spent the rest of the afternoon cleaning the generator and oiling the fans.

For supper they had cornflakes and the milk that Mr. Manoover had sent, which proved to be the richest, creamiest milk anyone had ever had. They picked sweet summer apples in the orchard, and nearly everyone agreed it was quite a good supper for a warm summer evening. Oggy said he preferred roast chicken.

By the time the crickets were all tuned up for the night, the children and Miss Shrubb had tucked themselves into their beds and had fallen asleep without a bit of trouble.

In the morning they washed in the brook, which was cold as snow and just as refreshing. Mr. Manoover had quietly come and gone, leaving them a dozen fresh eggs and another can of milk. Murk and Oggy dug a hole and built a small fire, and Miss Shrubb cleverly used an empty tin can to boil the eggs, which were eaten with the rest of yesterday's bread spread with jam.

The children took the few plates and cups to the brook, and Miss Shrubb showed them how they could be cleaned by rubbing them thoroughly with sand and rinsing them many times in clear water.

"Now," said Arabella, when everything was in order, "it's time to start the chain of events which will determine our fate."

"Oh, for Pete's sake, Arabella!" said Oggy, showing his usual impatience with Arabella's syntax.

"Please don't be so mysterious, Arabella," complained Melinda. "What events? What fate?"

"Well, we can't plan *too* far ahead," said Arabella, impervious to criticism, "but right now it seems to me we have to decide what we really want to do."

Miss Shrubb and ZoZo braided long ropes of grass, while Murk chewed on a piece and thought about the problem. Oggy seemed to think better blowing softly on the oboe. Melinda just stared at Arabella as if trying to see through to her hidden thoughts.

"Well," said Murk finally, "we want Miss Shrubb to be safe. That's first."

"That's right," Oggy agreed, "but besides that, we want to have a pretty good time before we have to go back and get . . . get punished."

"We don't want to be punished at all!" cried Melinda.

"No," said Arabella, "and that's a problem."

"It's all a problem, except for having fun," said Oggy.

"Not really," said Arabella. "It's not too hard when you think about it. Miss Shrubb, for instance. I think I can see a solution to *that*." Everyone looked at Arabella with interest. "We know what we think is right, don't we?" Everyone nodded. "Then all we have to do is stay hidden and send a message saying we won't come back unless they leave Miss Shrubb alone. That's all."

"That's all!" exclaimed Miss Shrubb. "Arabella, that's very handsome of you, but it's entirely too drastic. I wouldn't want to put you in that position. I shall just have to give myself up if it comes to that."

"No!" cried Murk. "Besides," he added shrewdly, "you're just being selfish that way."

"Selfish?" asked Miss Shrubb, mystified.

"Yes," said Arabella, catching Murk's eye. "Murk's right. What about your marsh if you give yourself up?"

Miss Shrubb's sweet face saddened. "Ah!" she said.

"But why would that idea work?" asked Oggy. "I mean I really don't understand that. Look, we say we aren't coming back unless they leave Miss Shrubb alone. Right? But it's our parents who want us home, and it's the Mayor who is after Miss Shrubb."

"Yes," said Arabella, "but your parents vote for the Mayor. They will just have to use pressure on him."

"Our parents and the rest of the town," said Murk.

"The rest of the town votes for the Mayor, too."

"Then," Arabella said, "we may have to involve the rest of the town, too." She shivered.

"But do they care?" asked Oggy. "Do they care anything about Miss Shrubb? I'm sorry . . ." he said to Miss Shrubb. "I didn't mean . . ."

"That's all right." Miss Shrubb smiled. "You're right, of course. I doubt if the people know enough about me or the marsh to care if I go back."

"Or even care to know," mourned Arabella. "That's the trouble. But maybe we could tell them."

"Well, we could try," said Murk. "At least we could try."

"But how?" asked Oggy.

"Well, the first thing is to get this tree house into the air and go and talk to them," Arabella decided, springing to her feet.

"No!" cried Oggy. "We can't do that now."

"Why not?" Arabella asked.

"We just *can't!*" said Oggy, his face quite white and his expression intense. "Don't you see? I can't go back now. I was away half the day, and now all of the night. *I'm not supposed to be out of the yard.* Listen"— he turned to Murk—"could we go somewhere? Somewhere far. Canada!"

"Naw," said Murk. "Where'd we get all that gasoline?"

"We could do it," said Oggy. "We could come down in different places and earn money. We *could*." He looked eagerly at each of the children and Miss Shrubb. "And Miss Shrubb would be safe, too. See, it would all be great! We could do it."

"Maybe we could," agreed Arabella, "if we had to. But why should we?" she asked in a reasonable tone. "It's safe in this cornfield. We have everything we need right here. And we can have a very nice vacation, too. At the same time, we can keep Miss Shrubb away from the marshals until we get things straightened out."

"That's right Oggy," Murk said. "This is really fine right here."

"Listen," said Oggy, "it's my house. Remember that! You can't boss me around in my house. You can't even get on it without my invitation. *And I say we go to Canada!*"

Melinda grabbed Miss Shrubb's arm nervously. Arabella and Murk stared at Oggy. Finally Arabella said, "Okay, Oggy. It's your house. Take it. Go on. We'll stay here. We'll be all right." She turned her back.

"I must go with Oggy in flying house," ZoZo said

sadly. "Good-bye, white horse." And he climbed aboard.

Oggy climbed aboard, too. He looked at the generator switch. He turned it on and it clacked noisily. He tested the tilt of the fan blades, examined the rudder fan. Then he stood quietly coiling a length of rope. He coiled it, and coiled it, and coiled it, his back turned to the children in the cornfield. Then he turned off the motor.

"Okay," he said. "I'll stay." And he jumped down from the tree house and started busily to braid grass. ZoZo came and sat beside him.

Arabella released the breath she seemed to have been holding, and Murk said, "Okay, that's great," just as Mr. Manoover arrived in the field.

"We thank you for the beautiful eggs," Miss Shrubb said to him as he came puffing up.

Mr. Manoover blushed. "Don't thank me, but them hens," he said. "Very good hens. Say," he said, "you people are in the newspapers!" and he took a crumpled paper out of his pocket.

"Ooooh," cried Melinda, "we're really Very Important. Let's see."

Arabella had already whipped the paper from Mr.

Manoover's hand and was scanning the front page. " 'Goodbury Children Take Off in Flying Machine,' " she read aloud. "That's the headline."

"Flying machine!" exclaimed Murk. "Oh, boy!"

"Go on, Arabella," urged Oggy.

" 'Five children from Goodbury disappeared today' —that's yesterday—'after mysteriously gaining altitude in a strange flying craft. Reports vary as to the nature of this craft, although a parent of one of the children, Mr. Clarence Clay, said it was a tree house. However, this is unconfirmed. No information as to the destination of the craft is known, nor is the purpose of the flight. However, there are abundant rumors. The children involved in the disappearance are'—and then it gives our names," finished Arabella.

"Ooooh!" cried Melinda. "Look at that! My name is in the newspaper. Oh, my, I'm glad I came."

"Well," said Arabella, "it's publicity, anyway. Come on, let's get going."

Mr. Manoover looked anxious. "Yer comin' back?" he asked anxiously.

"Of course," said Arabella. "We have to go off on a mission, but we'll be back soon."

"I wish I could go on a mission," said Mr. Manoover.

"Perhaps you can sometime," said Murk. "Couldn't he, Arabella?"

"Not impossible," said Arabella, "if everything goes well."

"Listen," said Murk to Mr. Manoover, "could you look up and down the road and all around and see if there's anyone about? It's important that no one sees us near the field."

"You be the lookout," said Oggy.

Mr. Manoover responded to the responsibility. He went through the field and looked up and down the road, here and there, hither and yon, including up.

He was just about to turn his back to the road when a car came tearing along, tires squealing on the curve. When the driver saw Mr. Manoover, he jammed on the brakes and brought the car to an abrupt stop . . . so abrupt that Mr. Manoover imagined for a moment that the back of the car had bucked into the air. A head poked out from the back window, and a head poked out from the front window. Mr. Manoover recognized the town marshals.

"Have you seen them?" both heads asked.

Mr. Manoover never answered quickly, and most particularly if he was suspicious. He was suspicious now. He reached over and plucked an immature bean from a vine and chewed it slowly. Delicious. He looked back at the car. The heads were jerking around impatiently, the mouths moving again.

"Hey!" yelled the one in the back, "did you see this bunch of school kids from Goodbury? Flying around in a tree house, they are." As soon as it had said the words, the head looked abashed.

"Flyin' around?" Mr. Manoover considered this. "No," he said slowly, "there's no one flyin' around

here. No one at all." And he looked up and scanned the empty sky, as if to check the fact.

"Well, keep your eyes open," said the head in front. "These kids' parents are pesterin' the police and everyone in the town hall to do somethin'. *Do* somethin'! How am I supposed to catch kids flyin' around! With a lasso?" He roared at the idea, and they were off.

Mr. Manoover watched them out of sight, checked the road again, and then went back to the cornfield. "Your society got any enemies?" he asked. "There do seem to be some folks out after you."

The children looked concerned. "Don't you worry," said Mr. Manoover proudly. "I lied to 'em. I lied to 'em by sort of telling the truth. I just said no one is flying around. And no one is . . . right now."

"Is that the kind of lying you do?" asked Miss Shrubb.

"That's one kind," said Mr. Manoover. "I can do others if need be."

"Well, if it's all clear now, let's get going," said Arabella.

"Okay," said Murk. "All aboard, and let's cast off." He started the generator, which clattered steadily without missing a beat, and shifted the big fan into low.

Then, as Mr. Manoover rechecked the road, Murk tilted the blades to the up position, and they were flying again. They waved to Mr. Manoover, who waved back enthusiastically.

The tree house rose slowly, straight up, until it was slightly above the height of the trees. Then Murk called to Oggy, "Okay, now push the blades to the forward position." Oggy, by now a competent first mate, did just that, and the tree house started to move toward the orchard. Everyone settled into a comfortable position after the slight tension of the take-off.

"Oh, this is just like a vacation!" said Melinda. "Really, it's just grand!"

Oggy advanced the big fan to high speed, and using the rudder fan, Murk steered them out over the meadow. As they crossed the road, some people, walking along, looked up and pointed excitedly.

"Don't worry about them," said Arabella. "It doesn't matter now if they see us, as long as they don't see our landing field. And now, we have more important things to think about."

"What things?" asked Melinda.

"Strategy," said Arabella. "In the first place, Miss

Shrubb, you had better stay hidden in the house until we size up the situation."

"Really, Arabella," said Miss Shrubb, "you are such a comfort. You do have your wits about you."

"In the second place," Arabella went on, "we must all be quite firm and . . . and dignified."

"We're coming into town," said Murk, and he steered the tree house toward the town square. It was empty.

"You forgot it was Sunday," said Oggy to Arabella, disgustedly. "Everyone's in church." At which moment, the doors of three churches opened, and suddenly the empty town square was quite full of Sunday-dressed people, all looking up and pointing.

Murk crisscrossed the square several times while the children and the astonished populace of Goodbury exchanged stares.

"Oh, that's enough exhibitionism," said Arabella. "We'd better see if we can find our parents." Oggy crouched nervously inside the door of the tree house.

It wasn't hard to find them. Grouped into an anxious knot, the children's parents were frantically waving and trying to get their attention. By fixing the fan blades so that they neither raised nor lowered the craft, nor moved it forward or back, Murk was able to bring the tree house to a hovering position above the spot where they stood. He shut off the rudder fan and turned the top fan to low speed.

"Now what?" he asked Arabella.

Arabella came to the railing and looked down into the familiar faces below. They looked somehow less familiar from this angle, and their behavior was uncharacteristic.

"Oh, gosh!" cried Oggy, shrinking way back. "There's my mother."

Mrs. Serafin was shouting, as, indeed, they all were. "Arabella! Arabella! Are you all right?"

"Isn't that interesting," Arabella remarked. "Notice the change? 'Are you all right?' not, 'Come down this minute!'"

"We're fine, Mother," called Arabella. "We're all just fine."

Mrs. Rose, a dainty woman, looked quite tearful. "Melinda!" she called. "Oh, Melinda, dear, we were so worried about you."

"But we told you yesterday," said Melinda, "there's nothing to worry about."

"Nothing to worry about!" Mr. Rose stepped forward. "Do you children realize what you are doing?

Why that thing could fall out of the sky any minute."

"Not a chance," said Murk. "It's very airworthy," he added proudly.

"Well, that's not the point, anyway," said Mr. Serafin, pushing his way to the front of the crowd. "Whether or not it's safe, *it's out of the question*. Now, get on down here this instant!"

Just then a very distinguished, dark gentleman, dressed all in white, came out of the group. "You are coming down," he said firmly. "I am accustomed to being obeyed. I am Ambassador from Peroque. I am having my son take away. Not good."

"Look, Papa!" cried ZoZo. "I am flying in flying house. You buy me flying house? Yes?"

Mr. Clay called, "Listen, Oggy, this is a very nasty thing. Why it's even in the newspapers!"

"And on the radio!" moaned Mrs. Rose.

Mrs. Kitt was sobbing, but Mr. Kitt called sternly. "Look here, Murk, what's this all about? What are you kids up to? What do you want?"

"Ah!" said Arabella thoughtfully. "There it is again! My father said that yesterday. 'What do you *want?*' There seems to be more to this than meets the eye."

The parents drew themselves back into a knot and started talking among themselves, occasionally pointing up and shaking their heads.

Mrs. Clay detached herself from the group. "Oggy," she called tearfully. "Oggy, dear, you bring that tree house down now, dear."

Mr. Serafin now came forward, a new and pleasant smile replacing the frown of a few moments ago. "Tell you what, Arabella," he called. "We know you are anxious to go on a vacation, but that's no way to do it. But you come down now, and we'll sit down and talk about it." Arabella shook her head.

"And listen, Arabella," Mrs. Serafin chimed in, "we're talking about getting that big new encyclopedia you wanted."

"Wow!" said Arabella. "They're *bribing* us! They really do want us to come down. And that *is* a temptation."

"Hey, I don't want an encyclopedia," said Oggy.

"Neither do I," said Melinda.

"But you do want *something*," said Arabella slowly.

"Sure," said Murk. "Everybody does."

"What?" asked Arabella. "I mean what important . . . that you couldn't get . . . on the ground?"

"Gee, I don't know right off," Murk said.

"I want flying house," cried ZoZo.

"Go on, Arabella," Melinda urged, "tell them about Miss Shrubb now."

But Arabella had a strange look on her face. She raised her hand warningly. "No, wait!" she exclaimed. "This is important. I am just beginning to see what the possibilities of this situation are, what the purpose is. No! Let's not tell them about Miss Shrubb just yet. Let's just . . ." She turned to the people below and cupped her hands around her mouth.

"Parents and friends," she called at the top of her voice. Everyone fell silent. "As you can see, we are quite safe and perfectly well and happy. We don't wish to cause you any anxiety. Really. However, we can't come down at the moment." A hard look came onto her sharp little face. "We ask you not to try and pursue us, or you will force us to fly far away and hide."

Oggy's face brightened at this intriguing thought. "Oh, boy!" he said.

Arabella continued. "But, if you do not harass us, we will return tomorrow . . . with our terms."

The children regarded Arabella with surprise. "Terms!" said Murk. "Hey, Arabella!"

"Terms!" Mr. Serafin shouted. "Arabella! What do you think you are?"

"I think I am a child," said Arabella, "who finds herself in a position to influence adults." Mr. Serafin considered this.

The Ambassador from Peroque stepped forward. "I go to Washington," he shouted. "This is international incident."

"Oh, dear," cried Melinda. "We were supposed to make him *like* Americans."

"Come on, Murk," Arabella said hastily, "I think this is the dramatic moment. Let's leave now."

Murk quickly adjusted the fans, switched on the rudder fan, turned the tree house eastward, and started off over the town hall. Mr. Serafin, Mr. Kitt, and some of the townspeople tried running along on the ground to follow them, but buildings and walls soon slowed them down and they fell hopelessly behind.

The children looked back at the parents standing with heads turned skyward, eyes shaded. Melinda said, "I feel sorry for them."

"So do I," said Oggy.

"But why are we *doing* it if we're sorry?" asked Melinda.

"Because, silly," Arabella said, *"we are committed!"*

11

A Position of Influence

"We had better double back and zigzag a bit if we don't want anyone to see which way we are going," said Murk.

"That's a good idea," agreed Oggy, "and then we can dodge in behind the woods and approach the farm from the other side. That should confuse 'em."

"This is sort of fun," said Melinda. "Like a game."

Miss Shrubb came out of the house then and sat down on the bench. "My goodness!" she said. "I really am so out of touch with everyday things that I don't quite know how to judge this, but it does seem to me that this whole situation is very extraordinary."

"Well, we are in a very peculiar position," said Arabella, by way of explanation.

"Boy, are we ever!" said Oggy, fearful again.

"That's it," agreed Arabella. "You see, I suddenly realized we stand to lose face when we get back. I mean they may be willing to offer us encyclopedias and things to get us down, but we are still the 'bad guys.' We are guilty. We have harbored a fugitive, kidnaped the Ambassador's son . . ."

"And run away from home!" added Oggy.

Melinda started to sob. "Ooooh, I don't want to be guilty."

"Exactly," said Arabella. "It's perfectly human not to want to feel guilty. You don't have to feel bad about that. The thing is to work it so that we don't have to feel guilty."

"But how?" sobbed Melinda.

"Look," said Arabella, using a freezing cold voice, "they were trying to bribe us. Right? They were offering a kind of ransom, even though we hadn't even asked for anything. Well, then, *let's* ask for something . . . but for something *big!* For heaven's sake! When are we ever going to be in a position like this again?"

Oggy's eyes opened wide with anticipation. Murk and Miss Shrubb just stared at Arabella.

Melinda stopped sobbing long enough to ask, "But

how will that make us any less guilty?" and then started to sob again.

"It all depends on what we ask for," said Arabella. She was thoughtful for a moment. "It has to be something enormous. Something worthwhile."

ZoZo said, "I think, I ask for tree house *and* a white horse."

"What I'd really like," said Murk slowly, "I mean *really* like . . . is a big metal lathe for my workshop. That's what I really want."

Melinda snuffed her tears to a halt. "I want . . ." she said, smiling for the first time since they left the square, "I want a long evening gown, a pink one, with silver shoes."

Oggy said, even before Melinda had finished, "What I'd like is a trip around the world . . . the whole world. That's what I'd like."

"Oh, yes!" Arabella nodded, forgetting, for a moment, her own train of thought. "That *would* be marvelous! But no. No, that's not the kind of thing. We have to ask for something kind of magnificent . . . like something that can do other people some good, too. Otherwise we're still just selfish and guilty. See?"

"Like what?" Murk asked.

"Maybe a concert hall," said Oggy. "How about we take a long trip first, and then, when we come back, we get them to build a big concert hall."

"How about school only twice a week?" Murk suggested. "We'd be popular then, for sure."

But Arabella was hardly listening. Her eyes were focused on the far horizons revealed to them by the flying tree house. "Listen," she said, not bringing her eyes back. "Listen, do you remember the other day when we were talking about what a mess the grown-ups made of the world?"

"Oh, sure," said Oggy. "I remember. You said *you* could do it better."

"Well let's!" said Arabella, looking from face to face now. "Let's tell them how to fix things. And let's make them do it!"

"Do *what?*" asked Murk. "And how are you going to make them do it?"

Arabella's mind was racing. "We have to talk it over," she said. "We have to decide just what the best thing is. But if we do something fine, we'll be heroes instead of villains. Can't you see that? And they'll do it! They'll do it because we'll stay here until they do. And they want us down."

"My mother wants me down," said Oggy. "But

I still can't see why the townspeople should care."

"We have to make them care," said Arabella. "Anyhow, it's an international incident. Didn't you hear the Ambassador say so? As soon as he starts to complain to the government, we're going to have a lot more attention."

"Complain to the government!" Melinda wailed. "Ohhhhh!"

"Oh, do shut up and stop that howling, Melinda," Arabella snapped.

Melinda stopped and stared sadly at Arabella. "Oh, Arabella!" she breathed reproachfully.

Murk steered the tree house behind the small woodland, doubled back again, to confuse anyone who might see them, and approached Mr. Manoover's field from the other side. Then, with Oggy adjusting the fan blades, Murk brought the craft in for a perfect landing. "Safe as a corn weevil," he said, with a great deal of satisfaction, and hopped out into the field to stretch his legs.

Mr. Manoover had left them a small pile of supplies. Miss Shrubb went over to examine them. "Why," she said, "this is a hot, fresh-baked loaf of bread." She sniffed it. "Oh, my! What a beautiful gift!" Besides the bread, there was a big bowl of cottage cheese. "That will be a nourishing lunch," Miss Shrubb said.

Oggy went off to get water from the well, and Murk went cautiously to the vegetable garden where he pulled a few carrots. And even if the lunch was nourishing, it was tasty in a way that food at home never seemed to be. When they had finished every crumb of the hot bread and every curd of the cottage cheese, they went down to the brook to wash up. There was a willow beside the brook which offered green shade, and Melinda said she thought it would be a good place to nap.

"Not now," said Arabella. "Now we have to work out a plan, but it would be a great place for a meeting." So Melinda reluctantly gave up the idea of a nap, and the children arranged themselves under the willow for a meeting.

"Now," said Arabella, "let's consider what we can do that's important . . . so important that it will help everybody." She waved her arms at the whole world.

"But you can't do something for *everybody*," complained Murk. "Nobody can do something for everybody, even if they wanted to."

"We can try," said Arabella a trifle impatiently.

"We're doing something very risky, and it's going to
have to be worth it."

"But what kind of thing?" asked Melinda.

"Well," said Arabella, thinking, "what needs im-
proving most for children?"

"Grown-ups!" said Oggy without hesitation.

Arabella looked interested. "All right, let's consider
the major crimes that adults commit."

"Crimes!" exclaimed Miss Shrubb. "*Really,* Arabella!"

"Well, maybe that *is* putting it too strongly," agreed Arabella. Anyhow, one of the worst things is tyranny, of course."

"What's tyranny exactly?" asked Oggy.

"Absolute rule," said Arabella, "usually despotic, severe—for instance, the unreasonable and tyrannical behavior of Mayor Kronk to Miss Shrubb."

"Bossy-like?" asked Oggy.

"Yes, bossy, but more so," said Arabella.

"All right," said Oggy. "I'm against that. What else?"

"Consider," said Arabella, "the worst things they do. We can't take everything. Only the very worst."

"They're mean," said Melinda.

"How mean?" asked Miss Shrubb.

"My papa is mean," said ZoZo. "He not let me ride white horse in parade in my country."

"They make you do things you don't want to do," said Melinda.

"Yes," said Oggy. "That sort of thing. Make you eat cauliflower."

"I *like* cauliflower," said Melinda.

"Oh, for heaven's sake!" said Arabella. "We've been there before."

"They push you on the bus," said Oggy. "Sometimes they yell at people."

"They don't really pay attention to what you say," said Arabella.

"If I may venture something," said Miss Shrubb, "it sometimes seems to me from my small world in the marsh that people outside just don't feel each other's troubles as we do in the marsh."

"Yes," said Arabella, "that's important. They're apathetic."

"There's so much," said Murk. "I'm *always* thinking of something grown-ups are doing to make things harder, but now I can't seem to think of much except one thing."

"What's that?" asked Oggy.

"The worst thing they do—the very worst thing— is have wars."

Everybody stared at Murk. Then Arabella said very softly, "Oh, Murk!" And then she said very fast, "Look! They are going to *have* to listen to us now. I think maybe we will not ask for just *one* thing. I think we will ask for . . . oh . . . three things! We'll say that we will come down if they will do three things."

"Ooooh!" said Melinda. "That's just like a fairy

story—the king gives the brave knight three tests, or three wishes, or three . . ."

"Why three?" asked Murk.

"We can't be too greedy," said Arabella.

"Well, what *are* the things?" asked Oggy.

"We'll have to talk it out and vote, of course," said Arabella. "But we can start in easy and make them agree to one thing at a time. Then we build up. *Then* we hit them with the clincher."

The children sat quietly under the willow, considering the project. Oggy asked, "But is this . . . well, all right to do?"

"Well, it may smack a bit of criminality, but the purity of its purpose will justify it."

"I wish I could understand half of what you say, Arabella," complained Melinda.

"But do you suppose it really could work?" asked Miss Shrubb.

"Why not?" said Arabella. "Up to now we have been dependent, utterly dependent. We have had to play it their way. But now, for the first time in our lives, we are in a position of power. I wouldn't be surprised if we could change the world!"

"Oh, Arabella!" said Miss Shrubb.

12

A Plan Grows
in a Cornfield

Oggy spent the rest of the afternoon running arpeggios and scales on the oboe. The cornstalks moved slightly in the breeze, and the light sound of the oboe rose above them. Mrs. Manoover, up in the house, stopped now and then in her sweeping and thought she heard a bird whose song she nearly recognized. It just escaped her recollection.

Arabella sat under the willow and re-read Winston Churchill, while Melinda napped. Murk made a fishing net out of his shirt, waded in the brook, and caught three trout. ZoZo spent the time riding the white horse through the paths of the little woods. Miss Shrubb found it possible to weave some very attractive and useful egg baskets out of corn husks. When Mr. Manoover appeared in the late afternoon she presented the baskets to him.

He was quite flustered and pleased. "Mighty nice," he said. "I thank you."

"And thank you for the delicious bread and cheese," said Miss Shrubb. "Truly delicious!"

"Missus bakes a fine loaf of bread," said Mr. Manoover. "Thought for a minute she'd notice a loaf was gone, but she made eight loaves and didn't seem to miss the one."

"We've got some trout for our supper," said Murk. "We can make a little fire and cook 'em quickly on a stick."

"You could roast a few ears of corn, too, if you want," said Mr. Manoover. "Help yerself."

"And will you join us?" asked Miss Shrubb.

"Well, I can't stay away from the house too long," said Mr. Manoover, "but I'll come out after my supper and have a word or two with you when I do my evening chores." And then he scooted into the cornfield and disappeared among the rows.

Miss Shrubb and Murk cleaned the fish; Arabella and Oggy and ZoZo went to gather wood; Melinda set the table. Then they built a small fire, and while it was burning down a bit they gathered some young ears of corn from the rows close to the clearing. Mr. Manoover had told them just to throw the ears into the fire, husks and all. Then they put the trout on forked sticks and broiled them until they were done.

When dinner was over, Mr. Manoover came and joined them, and they all sat around the fire and stared into the embers. Miss Shrubb said softly, "If you stare deeply enough into the fire, you can see the truth."

"What do you see?" asked Oggy, straining his eyes and trying to construct a vision in the embers.

"Oh," said Miss Shrubb, "I always see real things, important things—kindness, things like that." And then she quickly changed the subject and said to Mr. Manoover, "That was delicious corn. The most delicious I ever ate."

Mr. Manoover smiled with pleasure. "Thank you," he said. "I do believe you are the first person to tell me so. Do you have any idea how many people in Meredith County eat this fine corn every year? Hundreds! And I doubt there are two or three have any idea I grew it for them, or what fine corn it is. Oh, how I would like to tell them all one day!"

"Maybe you can," said Arabella. "Maybe we can work it into the secret society's plans."

"Well, I surely would like that," said Mr. Manoover. "And I would surely be honored if the society worked it into its plans, I can tell you that. Yes I would."

They fell silent again, staring at the embers. Little bursts of flame shot up now and again, and for a moment they were sharply revealing. They separated the real from the unreal. All that was within the circle of light was true; everything outside it was a fantasy.

Suddenly Arabella broke the silence. "Mr. Manoover, is there a radio in your house?"

"Yes," said Mr. Manoover. "But I can't take it out. Missus wouldn't like it. But hey, I have an old one in the barn. Only it doesn't work very well."

"Maybe I could fix it," said Murk.

So Mr. Manoover, Miss Shrubb, and the children slipped through the back door of the barn, and Mr. Manoover lit a small electric bulb which threw a very thin yellow light over everything. The barn was in an extraordinary disorder. It was quite wonderful that Mr. Manoover was able to find the radio at all. It was on a low shelf with some old nuts and bolts, two broken cow-medicine bottles, six broken harness buckles, a spindle of bills, all well hidden behind a small heap of hay and well hung with spider webs.

Murk puttered around with the radio for a while, tightening screws, cleaning connections, cutting and rejoining wires; and then, finally, a very squawky voice was heard on the Meredith station. "Fifteen thousand troops fought today in the jungles of . . ."

"Did he say fifteen or fifty?" asked Oggy.

"That's it!" exclaimed Arabella. "Fifteen or fifty! They're just numbers instead of people . . . real people."

The radio announcer's voice was crackling and squawking again, sparked with sharp tattoos of static. "Here at home," he said, "interest is growing in the strange disappearance, reappearance, and redisappearance of the five children from Goodbury."

"That's us!" exclaimed Oggy.

"National interest is coming to bear on the matter now, since it appears that there may be international implications to the affair."

Melinda uttered a cry.

"Hush," said Arabella.

The announcer's voice continued: ". . . a protest lodged with the State Department by Mr. Ortega Sejura, Ambassador from Peroque. An Assistant Attorney General is coming to Goodbury tomorrow to speak with the Ambassador and to the other parents involved. A radarscope, in nearby Southbury, showed an unidentified flying object at a low altitude, but a search of the area by the sheriff's office has revealed no clue to the children's whereabouts. Attempts to follow them, after their appearance today, failed. It is suspected they may have found a cave in the mountains."

"Hey, what a great idea!" exclaimed Oggy.

"More news on this as we get it. And now a look at sports . . ."

As the announcer said, "And now a look . . ." the barn door was thrown open, and the moonlight revealed a middle-aged lady in a bathrobe.

"Missus!" hissed Mr. Manoover, and in a quick motion threw several large forkfuls of hay over the children's heads.

"Sam Manoover," said Mrs. Manoover in a deep and rather challenging voice. "What are you doing in there?"

"Well," said Mr. Manoover, forking a bit more hay and thinking fast as he did it, "I'm doing two things. I've been trying to fix this old radio, see." He pointed to the radio, which was still squawking. "Besides that, I'm looking through this here hay for a mouse nest."

"Mouse nest!" squealed Mrs. Manoover, drawing her robe up over her knees.

"Yes, ma'am. Thought I saw a mess of mice leaping out of that hay there."

"Well," said Mrs. Manoover hurriedly, "it's getting late. You had better put out that lantern and come up to the house."

"I shall," said Mr. Manoover, just as a loud sneeze came from beneath the hay.

"What was that!" exclaimed Mrs. Manoover, stepping into the barn.

"Maybe I'm gettin' a cold," said Mr. Manoover. "A-choo!"

"Hurry up!" said Mrs. Manoover, and started out of the barn, as a whole chorus of sneezes erupted from the hay. "Achoo, achoo!" improvised Mr. Manoover.

"I'll have a mustard plaster ready for you," called Mrs. Manoover, "and some cough medicine."

"Oh, gosh!" said Mr. Manoover. "Now I'll have to suffer. Well, at least we didn't get caught!" he said as he pulled the hay off the children's heads.

"Ooooh, I itch!" complained Melinda. "Is there really a mouse nest in there?"

"Shouldn't surprise me," said Mr. Manoover.

"I am very itch, too," said ZoZo.

"Never mind that," said Arabella. "It's a very slight price to pay. Thank you," she said to Mr. Manoover.

"You better get out of here now," said Mr. Manoover. "I'll see you all in the morning with some fresh milk and a few eggs."

"Good night," they called.

"Hey," said Oggy, "where's Miss Shrubb?"

"Where's Miss Shrubb?" repeated Murk.

"She did come to the barn with us, didn't she?" asked Arabella. "I was so wrapped up in the radio, I didn't really notice."

Mr. Manoover picked up some hay. "Here she is," he said. "She's fallen asleep." Melinda came over and shook Miss Shrubb gently. "Wake up, Miss Shrubb, dear," she said.

Miss Shrubb sat up in the hay, looking more than ever like a bird in the nest. "Oh, dear," she said. "It's been such an exciting day, I must have dozed off. Do forgive me. Did I miss anything?"

"Only that we are national celebrities," said Arabella. "An Assistant Attorney General is coming to Goodbury to look into our disappearance."

"Oh, that's terrible!" said Miss Shrubb.

"Why?" asked Arabella. "It seems good to me. Very good. I was sure our parents were going to listen to us. I was fairly sure that certain other people in Goodbury were going to have to listen to us. But now, I think the whole *country* is going to have to listen to us. I would say everything is going along very nicely."

That night they lay in their cots and haystacks and on their air mattresses, calling back and forth to each other as new ideas for their plan occurred to them. Arabella even sat up suddenly in the middle of the night to think out another thought. The plan was a good one.

13

The Third Flight

In the morning, after a breakfast of fresh eggs and fresh milk, Miss Shrubb took an unusually firm tone with the children. It took them a bit by surprise. "We're all rather dirty," she said, "and it is a lovely sunny morning. I can wash out all your things and they will be dry in no time."

"Ahhh!" said Oggy. "I thought we had gotten away from all that stuff."

Miss Shrubb looked surprised. "Why, surely," she said, "it is not necessary to break away from all convention."

"Well, I wouldn't mind clean clothes," said Melinda. "I still itch from all that hay. But how? We have nothing to wear while our clothes are being washed."

"Here," said Miss Shrubb. "I can do two people's things at a time. In the meanwhile those two can wear my extra skirts. Fasten them around your necks . . . like this."

So, for the next couple of hours, the children took turns looking like a pair of tents, wearing Miss Shrubb's skirts from the neck down. And Miss Shrubb did a splendid job of scrubbing out all the clothes and drying them on sun-baked rocks, where they smoothed out fairly well. The boys protested a bit about the skirts, but they were so amused at each other's appearance that they rather enjoyed it after all. And when they were all washed clean in the brook and dressed in their sun-dried clothes, they were surprisingly refreshed and thanked Miss Shrubb for her efforts.

"Now," said Arabella, "we are ready for our negotiations. Murk, is the tree house ready to fly?"

"Oh, good!" exclaimed ZoZo, immaculate again in his white suit. "We go once more in flying house. Very good. I like."

"It's all ready," said Murk. "It's full of gasoline and all tuned up."

"Before we go, though," said Arabella, "is there some way we could make a megaphone or something? All that yelling is hard."

"How about the tin can from the peaches?" said Murk. "That should do it." And he did a bit of hammering and shaping that produced a lopsided but adequate megaphone. Arabella tried it out. "Testing," she called. Her voice came trumpeting out.

"Shhhhh!" everyone exclaimed at once.

"But what are we going to do, Arabella?" asked Oggy.

"I think the best thing is just to be very simple and direct and state the case to as many people as will listen."

"But I still can't see why they should do what we want," Oggy persisted.

"They may have lots of different reasons," said Arabella. "That's the way history goes. People sometimes get together and do the right thing . . . some of them for the wrong reasons."

And so they all climbed aboard the tree house once more, and Murk started up the generator. It sounded fine. Then Mr. Manoover arrived to go through his elaborate lookout routine. When he waved the all-clear sign, Murk put the craft into a slow ascent and with Oggy and ZoZo operating the fan lever piloted the tree house to its usual altitude above the treetops.

"This time," Arabella said, "I think there is really no need for you to hide, Miss Shrubb. No need at all."

"Oh, that's fine," said Miss Shrubb. "I much prefer to stay out in the sunshine."

They flew over the woods and then out over the marshland. Miss Shrubb came to the railing to look down. "Ah, see my dear little ducks," she said, "but notice how well hidden most of the creatures are. That's one of the splendid things about the marsh. It is a kind of hiding place from some of the cruel predators."

"But not from selfish mayors and marshals," said Arabella angrily.

"Speak of the devil!" cried Oggy. "Look!" and he pointed to a car on the road that skirted the town dump. "There they are! The marshals!"

"Oh!" wailed Melinda. "Now we'll be caught!"

"Don't be silly," said Arabella. "What difference does it make? We're flying into town where everyone will see us. Just look how excited they are." The marshals had jumped out of their car and were standing among tin cans on the dump, pointing up and shaking their fists.

"Temper, temper!" shouted Murk as he steered the

tree house right over their heads. The rest of the children and Miss Shrubb stood by the railing and waved.

As they approached the center of town they could see the morning crowds of people going to work, going to market, going about their business. But all that soon changed, and heads were turned upward and arms pointed skyward.

"We're attracting a lot of attention," said Murk.

"Good!" said Arabella. "That's what we want. Murk, can you steer us somewhere near the town hall?"

"Sure," said Murk, giving the rudder fan a turn. "I can fly you within an inch of wherever you want to go."

First they circled one of the church towers a few times, and Oggy took the broom and, reaching way out, rang the church bells a few peals with the long handle. It was quite deafening, even above the clack of the generator and the *whirr* of the fans. Arabella thought it may have been only an illusion that the clanging church bell had the effect of turning the people in the square to statues.

"Look at them!" she exclaimed. "They're immobilized. Honestly! This is beyond their comprehension for some reason or other."

But if the people in the square were momentarily cast in stone, the Mayor was not. At the moment he was sitting in the town hall, explaining to the Assistant Attorney General that the whole thing really had nothing to do with the office of the Mayor. The clarion call of the bell, at such an odd time, brought him to his window. "There they are!" he exclaimed. "There are those troublesome children. Now's your chance to talk to them." And the Mayor threw open his window and waved his arms wildly. "Hey!" he shouted. "Hey!"

The children saw the Mayor waving, and Arabella said, "There's that old Mayor Kronk now. Let's fly over and talk with him."

With Murk at the rudder and Oggy at the fan-flaps, the tree house was brought to a hovering position just outside the Mayor's window. The *whirr*ing of the big fan made it necessary for the Mayor to shout until his face was perilously pink.

"Now look here!" he yelled. "There's someone very important here wants to talk to you . . . an Assistant Attorney General."

The Assistant Attorney General put his head tentatively out the window and nodded at the introduction. He had not had any experience in negotiations under these circumstances and was ill at ease. "How do you do," he said. "We are here to discuss with you the urgent necessity of your coming down." Then he looked carefully at the passengers of the tree house and said, "Just a minute." He turned back to the Mayor. "Who is the lady on board? Nothing was said about a lady. If there is a chaperone, perhaps there is no need for alarm."

The Mayor looked again and saw Miss Shrubb. "Oh, dear!" he exclaimed. "*There* she is!"

"What's the matter?" asked the Assistant Attorney General.

"I . . . er . . . I think I may know the lady. Her name is Miss . . . er . . . Miss Slubb, I think."

The Assistant Attorney General put his head out the window again and said, "This is all very irregular," and then he had an idea. "Do you have a pilot's license?"

"Me?" asked Murk.

"Yes," said the Assistant Attorney General.

"Not yet," said Murk.

"Ah!" said the Assistant Attorney General. "Well, then! It's simple," he said, turning to the Mayor. "There's a law to cover this. He's flying without a pilot's license, so just tell them to come down."

"Me?" said the Mayor.

"This is a local matter, at the moment," said the Assistant Attorney General. "It's your responsibility to enforce the law locally."

"Oh, well," said the Mayor, and he put his head out the window again. "Now look here," he yelled. "You are violating the law—flying without a license. And besides that"—he pointed at Miss Shrubb—"you are harboring a fugitive from the law, that Miss Snugg. So you come on down. Right now." And he drew his head in again, the color of good red cabbage.

Throughout this inter-window oratory Arabella sat cross-legged on the platform, listening. Finally, when the Mayor withdrew, she got to her feet and picked up the megaphone that Murk had made. She went to the railing, leaned over, ignoring the Mayor, and addressed the people below, who seemed finally to have returned to flesh and blood. Some thoughtful citizen had summoned the children's parents, who could now be seen gathered in the center of the square.

"People of Goodbury," Arabella called. "Parents. Friends. How we happen to be up here is not the question right now. The fact is that we are here." Everyone in Goodbury had his eyes on Arabella at this moment, but while it was a heady experience, she did not let it divert her. "A great many people are interested in our coming down—our parents, the Ambassador from Peroque, the Mayor, and the Assistant Attorney General. We are here now to tell you that, while we enjoy being up here very much and, indeed, would happily stay up much longer . . . indefinitely . . . we will come down." She took a deep breath. "We will come down on three conditions."

"Why, the little monsters!" said the Mayor, who just a moment before had been congratulating himself on his effectiveness as a law enforcer. "Three conditions!"

Arabella signaled to Miss Shrubb, who at first shook her head but then stood and joined Arabella at the railing. Arabella called to the crowd. "Many of you know Miss Shrubb. Perhaps you are wondering what Miss Shrubb is doing up here with us. Miss Shrubb had been evicted from her home. Miss Shrubb's home has been taken from her by the Mayor of Goodbury!"

At these words, the Mayor of Goodbury, leaning on his window sill, turned from red to purple and started to sputter to the Assistant Attorney General.

Arabella was going on. "The Mayor of Goodbury wants to use the marsh, which is Miss Shrubb's home, for something else, so he has turned Miss Shrubb out. Not only that, he has sent the town marshals after her." Arabella leaned over to see the effect of her words. Mouths were moving furiously and arms were gesticulating.

Miss Shrubb said to Arabella, "May I say something?"

"Oh, please!" cried Arabella and handed her the megaphone.

Miss Shrubb's tiny voice was amplified to all below. It sounded a bit like an old Victrola record, weak but clear. "Arabella has said," piped Miss Shrubb, "that my home is being taken from me—and that is true— but it is not the entire truth. A home is also being taken from thousands of wild creatures who depend on the marsh. And something is being taken from you —*all* of you—a cradle of life, a marsh full of wonders, a marsh full of marvels that most of us never know." Suddenly Miss Shrubb seemed surprised to find herself so articulate. She blushed and ducked her head and, thrusting the megaphone back at Arabella, scurried to the other side of the platform.

Arabella turned to Murk. "Murk," she said, "you tell them."

"Me!" protested Murk. "I can't do public speaking."

"Come on, Murk," said Oggy.

Murk took the megaphone and came slowly to the edge of the platform.

"Well, that's the thing," he called. "Just as Arabella and Miss Shrubb said. We're going to come down, but the first thing is Miss Shrubb has to be able to go back to the marsh . . . and *stay* there." He handed the megaphone back to Arabella and said, "Okay. I said it."

Arabella went back to her place at the railing. "That's the first condition," she called. "Just go to the Mayor and tell him you don't like his turning Miss Shrubb out, that you don't like the marsh being taken away from the creatures and from you. He has to do what you want him to, if you *say* so, because you are the people who vote for him. Okay. We'll listen to the radio tonight to hear what you have done. When it is done we'll be back with our second condition. Please don't try to follow us. Please don't force us to go far away. We will be true to our promises if you will be true to yours. Good-bye."

"Good-bye," yelled all the children, waving, and in the square many arms waved in answer.

"Wow!" said Arabella as the tree house turned in the direction of the countryside. "That makes me feel so . . . so powerful. I think I might have liked to have been an empress."

And, as they left the square, the marshal's car crept out of the crowd and followed them.

14

The Meeting, the Mayor, and the Marshals

In his office, a pink-through-purple Mayor was waving a clenched fist in the air. "Why, that's extortion!" he yelled, and then he turned to the Assistant Attorney General. "That's no flying machine," he fumed, "that's a blackmail machine! Innocent children! Innocent children, my foot!"

"Ah, well," said the Assistant Attorney General. "It's a little tempest, but my advice to you is to settle it at once. Now, my investigation shows that this is not a matter for the Attorney General's office, but I shall refer it to the Department of the Interior, because of the marsh business, and perhaps to the Aeronautics Board. Good day to you, sir."

Down in the square, the townspeople were forming into little caucusing knots, exchanging views. The parents of the children lost no time agreeing that the only possible thing to do was go and see the Mayor. Mr. Kitt said, "Yes, but we'll need the support of the other townspeople."

"Well, let's go around and talk to them, then," said Mr. Serafin, who was a natural executive. "You take the east side of the square, I'll take the west. You others can split up around the north and south of the square and talk to everyone." And that is just what they did. Before long the shifting groups of people took on the aspect of a square dance or a quadrille. Everyone disregarded what he had come to town for in the first place and concentrated completely on the matter at hand, except for a few who said, "This has got nothing to do with us," and went home.

"I don't let *my* kids tell me what to do," said a gentleman from Front Street.

"Nor do I," said his neighbor.

Mr. Serafin was the parent-representative at this caucus.

"Believe me when I tell you it is not usual for our children to tell us what to do either, but this is a very unusual case. It is extremely important that they come down. What they are doing may not be safe. Besides that, the Ambassador's son is on board. And besides that . . ." Mr. Serafin looked very thoughtful. "Perhaps it's *not* so bad to have them tell us what to do if what they say makes sense."

"But does it?" asked the hardware-store man. "What was it the Mayor was going to do with the marsh?"

"I heard," said the bakery man, "mark you, I only heard, that he was going to have a racetrack built."

"A racetrack!" exclaimed the man from Front Street. "Oh, boy!"

And the rumor sped around the square. There was strong sentiment to the effect that if the Mayor was planning to build a racetrack, the children in the tree house could look forward to flying around indefinitely.

Mr. Kitt was not having much more success. "But you don't see the real point," he said to his group. "It's not whether to have or not to have a racetrack. It's, first of all, the need to get these children down. Second, there *is* some merit in their proposition, if not in their manner of achieving it."

"Yeah, but a racetrack!" said a man from Second Street.

"Just a minute," said the department-store manager. "They built a racetrack in Eastham, and you know what? Half the people in town couldn't pay their bills! All their money was in the pockets of horses that lost. No, I'm not for a racetrack. I'll go to the Mayor with you."

"Thank you," said Mr. Kitt, a bit encouraged. "Well, if that's true, all of you merchants should be concerned, if only about your pocketbooks."

And a few heads did nod in agreement at that.

"Well, I'll go to the Mayor with you," the wife of the man from Second Street said suddenly. "With a racetrack in this town I'd never have enough money for a new refrigerator!"

Mrs. Rose and Mrs. Serafin were holding forth on the south side of the square. Mrs. Serafin was saying, "I don't really know too much about it, but I know that the marsh protects the higher land in many ways, and it's a spawning ground for seafood, besides being the home of all that wildlife."

Mrs. Rose said, "They say if you fill the marsh it affects the land and growing things for miles around. There aren't as many birds because there aren't as many nesting grounds and things for them to eat. Then, if there aren't as many birds, more insects are left to attack the crops, and then there isn't as much for us to eat . . . and so on. Something like that."

"Oh, dear," fretted one of the ladies, "it's like pulling a loose thread in a sweater."

Mrs. Kitt was wandering from group to group. "You remember poor Miss Shrubb," she said. "Such a harmless, nice little thing. And such pretty baskets. Let's not allow her to be put out of her home, no matter what else is done about this matter."

"Duck hunters unite!" Mr. Rose was calling. "Don't let your hunting grounds be destroyed."

At the end of an hour, a large pressure group was finally formed. They were joined in a common purpose but for different reasons.

"No racetrack," was their message to the Mayor because: There wouldn't be any money left to be spent in the town's stores if people gambled it at the racetrack; duck hunting, such as it was, would be spoiled; something about insects ruining the apple trees; and last, the homeless Miss Shrubb.

"All right!" cried the Mayor, covering his red ears with his pudgy hands to block out the clamor. "All right! If that's the will of the people, that's the will of the people. I only . . ." He smiled in what he hoped was an appealing manner. "I only wanted to make you happy. And let me add, this whole thing was suggested by the board of advisors, you know. No hanky-panky, you know."

"No one is accusing you of hanky-panky, Mr. Mayor," said Mr. Serafin.

"Now," said Mr. Kitt, "you'll have to notify the radio and newspapers so that the children will know that their request has been granted."

"Their *first* request," sighed Mr. Clay.

"All right," said the Mayor, but he wasn't paying attention anymore. He was busy thinking of some other scheme to win popularity.

While the Mayor was fighting a defensive battle in his office, his marshals were intent on conquest. When the tree house left the town square and started out over the houses and trees, the marshals had crept out of the crowd and headed quickly for the outskirts of town. The one driving the car alternated between watching the road and looking up through the front window. The second marshal had his head craned right out the back window, and he kept turning it as if it were on a swivel.

"There they go!" he shouted to the driving marshal, quite furious in his frustration.

As they skirted the bay, the children saw the marshals' car, and Oggy said, "Oh, gosh, if they get hold of us *now,* they'll give us a hard time. We've got to lose them."

Arabella said, "Well, we'll just have to lead them on a wild goose chase."

"I don't know," said Murk. "Right now, we're pretty close to Mr. Manoover's farm, and we could get there fast if we had to, but if we lead them on a chase we might . . ."

"We might what?" asked Melinda anxiously.

"We might run out of gas and not be able to get back," said Murk. Melinda began to cry.

"How long do you think we can stay up?" asked Arabella.

"I'm not sure," said Murk. "Maybe an hour or so."

"Okay," said Arabella. "Put the tree house into a hover, right out over the bay." Melinda cried harder, and Miss Shrubb began to comfort her.

Murk and Oggy brought the craft to a low hover

about five hundred yards from shore. On the shore, the marshals brought their car to a stop and got out.

Meanwhile, Arabella was tying the other length of venetian blind cord to the broom handle. She borrowed a hairpin from Miss Shrubb for a hook, baited it with bread and jam, and sat down to fish. Murk and Oggy grinned and sat down beside her.

Melinda stopped crying. "How is that going to help?" she asked.

"We just might be able to bore them to death," said Arabella.

As the minutes passed, there was complete silence and no movement on the tree house. Everyone sat or lolled about quite indolently. On the shore, the marshals, after standing perplexed for a while, sat down to watch.

When a half-hour had gone by, Murk said, "They're just going to sit there as long as we do, and *they* aren't going to run out of gas. We've got to do something else."

Suddenly Arabella cried, "I've got something on the line!" and they all helped her haul in a good-sized flounder.

"My word!" said Miss Shrubb. "I had no idea flounders liked bread and jam."

"Probably nobody ever offered it to them before," said Arabella. "What shall we do, Murk?"

"Well," said Murk, "the idea I have is this." And he told it, in a few words, to the horrified Miss Shrubb and the weeping Melinda. The others took it calmly.

In two minutes the rope ladder had been let down over the side, and Oggy and Murk were descending *into the bay*. Then they proceeded to swim in circles about the tree house, moving farther and farther away from it as they swam.

On the shore the somewhat sleepy marshals came to attention. Then they stood up. Then they took off their shoes. And *then* they started wading into the bay.

Oggy and Murk continued to swim around. On the tree house no one appeared to notice the marshals. The marshals, now up to their armpits, could no longer wade, so they began to swim. Oggy and Murk circled again. The marshals were well out into the bay.

Suddenly Murk yelled, "Okay, Arabella, start her up!" and he and Oggy began a fast sprint to the rope ladder. The marshals put on speed, too. Arabella

sprang to the rudder. Miss Shrubb stood ready at the fan lever.

It was slow, hard work for Murk and Oggy to pull themselves, soaking wet, up the rope ladder. Melinda and ZoZo crouched at the top, urging them on. Oggy came first, slowly, rung by rung, feeling as if he were weighed down with rocks. Murk hung on in the water, waiting for Oggy to get up. "Hurry up," he called. "They're getting awfully close!" Oggy reached the last rung and dragged himself over the railing. He fell, panting, to the platform. And now Murk was on the ladder.

"Start her moving, Arabella!" he cried.

"But you're not aboard yet," she protested.

"Never mind. Get going!"

And so, with the marshals only two arm lengths away, the tree house started to move out across the bay, with Murk holding onto the rungs of the rope ladder. He slowly pulled himself up the swinging ladder while Arabella kept the tree house moving as slowly and steadily as she could. When he was safely on board they all cheered, except Melinda, who cried.

Oggy and Murk rested, and Murk gave orders to Miss Shrubb and Arabella. "Switch the fan to high speed now," he said. "Give it a bit more tilt. Rudder to the left, Arabella." And with his backseat piloting, the craft was turned properly and headed in toward shore again. They passed right over the heads of the floundering marshals and waved.

As they approached the cornfield, the generator started to sputter. Murk jumped up and took the controls from Arabella. "Wow!" he said. "We got here none too soon." And with the generator stuttering and the fan acting a bit erratic, Murk lowered the tree house to its home place in the cornfield.

"Now," he said, "we know how long a tank of gas will last."

15

A Party in the Sky

"Listen," said Oggy later in the day, when they had recovered from the excitement of the trip from town. "We're taking an awful lot of things from Mr. Manoover, all because he thinks he belongs to a secret society."

"Well," Melinda said, "we really are a sort of secret society."

"Sort of," Oggy agreed. "But just by accident."

"I don't think he minds giving us the stuff," said Murk.

"Oh, he doesn't mind," said Oggy. "He likes it, maybe. But all the same, I think we should pay him."

"I think you are right, Oggy," Arabella said. "It isn't right for us to take all the food and gasoline and things unless we can repay him."

"But how?" asked Melinda. "We don't have any money."

"We could work," said Oggy.

"Help around the farm," said Arabella. "It's a good idea."

"Why don't we surprise him!" suggested Oggy. "We could get things done while he's wherever he is."

"I could tidy up that messy barn," said Melinda.

"I should like to help you do that," said Miss Shrubb.

"We'll have to stay out of sight of the house," said Arabella. "I believe I'll go and see if the vegetable garden needs weeding."

"I'm going to overhaul that old tractor of his," said Murk. "Want to help me, Oggy?"

"Sure I would," said Oggy.

"And I," said ZoZo, "I brush white horse."

When Mr. Manoover came into the barn at five o'clock, after an afternoon in the lower fields, he blinked his eyes several times to adjust to the dim light. When he could see, he didn't believe it anyway. "My word!" he exclaimed. "What could have happened?" The floor shone wetly, and around the edges of the barn were neat stacks of tools and wood. Boxes of nails, sorted by size, were on the shelves, and old harnesses were hung on pegs. The straw and hay were neatly confined to bins.

"Well!" he breathed. "That does beat all!" And he went out to pull some carrots for supper.

"Ah, now!" he cried when he saw clear signs of fresh hoeing and weeding. And then his eyes were drawn to the open shed behind the barn, where the old tractor always stood; but now, instead, there was something that looked like a brand new shining red machine. "Ah-h-h!" he exclaimed in wonderment. "What could have happened hereabouts?" But finding no answer, he pulled a few more carrots for Mrs. Manoover and then pulled some more for his guests, along with a few potatoes. Then he started down to the cornfield.

In the clearing, dinner was being prepared. Murk was holding the flounder over the coals, while Melinda and Arabella were setting the table.

"Here," said Mr. Manoover, "you can throw in these spuds and have some potatoes with your fish."

"Thank you," said Miss Shrubb, taking them and the carrots. "These fresh vegetables are a lovely treat." The sincerity of her thanks never failed to move Mr. Manoover. He had not quite got used to people appreciating his farm produce. He blushed.

"Listen," he said, "something very peculiar has happened. My barn's all swept up, my garden's weeded, and something has transformed my tractor." Puzzlement clouded his face.

"The children did it," said Miss Shrubb, not able to bear his discomfiture. "They thought you could use a little help."

"Well, say!" cried Mr. Manoover. "You did all that for me?"

"We're all members of the same society," said Oggy, by way of explanation. "It was a pleasure."

"Look at all *you* have done for us," said Melinda.

"Stay and have supper with us," said Arabella. "We're having this lovely fish."

"Well, because of Missus," said Mr. Manoover, "it would set her wondering—I'll not be able to say yes. I thank you, but I'm sorry."

"Well, we're sorry, too," said Miss Shrubb.

"May we go into the barn after supper and listen to the radio?" asked Arabella. "We're waiting for some news."

"Why, sure!" said Mr. Manoover. "I'll come in, too, after I've helped wash up." And he left them then, but reluctantly.

It wasn't long before certain aromas from the fire announced that the fish was only a little burned, and, with the blackened potatoes and the crisp carrots, it was eaten in a tired but somehow refreshing silence. Melinda invented fresh apple slices spread with peach jam for dessert, and everyone agreed that Melinda had invented something worthwhile.

The clean cool darkness of the barn was delightful and homey, and the hay, slightly wet, smelled like the country should. "This is a changed place," said Mr. Manoover as he came in. "But now, how am I going to find anything, with everything put away?"

They sat on a pile of straw, and Murk turned on the radio very low. There were several minutes of music, a long commercial announcement, and, finally: ". . . and now, the news. A committee of parents, conservationists, merchants, and duck hunters met with the Mayor of Goodbury today, in connection with the filling of Goodbury marsh. As a result of the meeting, the Mayor of Goodbury announced tonight that the marsh would remain undisturbed and its one human inhabitant would be allowed to return to her home."

At this point the children in the barn leaped up and

hugged each other and Miss Shrubb and Mr. Manoover, and jumped about congratulating each other. Mr. Manoover begged them to be quiet, so they retreated to a whispered joy.

They had missed whatever the radio announcer said next, but they heard him finish. "The parents of the five flying children have issued a plea through this station that the children return as quickly as possible."

"Hey, just what is it all about anyway?" asked Mr. Manoover, thoroughly confused by the news and the hugs.

"It's just that the good guys are ahead a little," said Arabella, "and it's a very nice feeling."

"Let's celebrate," said Oggy.

Melinda cried, "Oh, I wish I had my party shoes."

"Ooooh, a party!" exclaimed ZoZo.

"By the light of the moon," said Arabella. "Perfect!"

"I have a great idea," said Murk. "If I do say so myself," he added. "Let's have the party in the air."

"Why not?" said Arabella. "Come on!"

"Me, too?" asked Mr. Manoover doubtfully.

"Of course, you, too," said Murk, and they all raced out of the barn and through the vegetable garden into the cornfield.

The moon lit the field, spotlighting the tops of the cornstalks and giving a carnival feeling to the night. They lifted the camouflage from the roof of the tree house and climbed aboard. Mr. Manoover got on timidly. "Are you sure it's all right for me?" he asked.

"Of course," said Murk.

"Why not?" asked Oggy.

"I've never been off the ground," said Mr. Manoover. "Not once."

"High time," said Oggy. "Sit here on the bench. You'll enjoy it."

Mr. Manoover sat on the bench and ZoZo sat on one side of him and held one hand, while Melinda sat on the other side of him and held his other hand. Murk started the generator, now replenished with gasoline, Oggy took his place at the big fan lever, and they were off.

Slowly they rose on a beam of moonlight until they were at their normal cruising altitude. They flew across the cornfield, over the woods, and out over the marsh. Oggy and Murk set the controls to the hover position and relaxed.

"Well, my!" breathed Mr. Manoover when he was used to the sensation.

"Now," said Oggy, "let's have the party," and he took his oboe and started a very merry tune without anyone asking him to. All the feet on board tapped, and then Melinda jumped up and started to do a little jig. She turned and twirled and then hopped over and bobbed a curtsy to Murk. Murk shuffled a bit but gallantly got to his feet and joined Melinda. Mr. Manoover tapped his feet, and Miss Shrubb clapped her hands. Then ZoZo bowed to Arabella, and they joined the dance.

The dance wasn't over until they were all out of breath. "What next?" asked Murk.

"I can do my headstands and backflips," said Arabella.

"Fine," said Murk. So Arabella stood on her head for alarming minutes, and then spun some frightening backflips that had Miss Shrubb's and Melinda's hearts jumping.

"You'll backflip right off the platform, Arabella!" Melinda cried, and there were a few near misses which only added to the entertainment.

Then ZoZo took the center of the stage. He gave a stiff and formal bow and said, "Now I sing song from Peroque—a song about white horse, his master die

and cannot ride in parade. Very sad song." Whereupon he began to sing, in a sweet high voice and a
strange tongue, a song which held their interest though
they could not understand a word. When it was over,
Melinda was crying. ZoZo was pleased.

"It would be a perfect party," said Arabella, "if we
had something partyish to eat." Miss Shrubb became
alert.

"I wonder if you would care for some raspberry
ade?" she asked.

"Raspberry ade?" asked Arabella. "What is it?
Where would we get it?"

Miss Shrubb got up and walked into the tree house.
She rattled the cups and called, "Early this afternoon
I saw a lovely patch of raspberries, and I thought I'd
do something with them. I crushed them up and put
the juice in the water cooler. See if you like it."

Everyone sipped the strange drink cautiously, and
then enthusiastically. "Why, it tastes like summer!"
cried Arabella.

"That's it," said Miss Shrubb. "Just like it."

"This," said Mr. Manoover, after his third glass, "is
good enough to make a person give up medicinal
spirits."

Oggy picked up his oboe again and played something minor and melting to match the moonlight. They sprawled about on the platform in complete restfulness.

But Melinda said, "Don't you feel just a little homesick though?"

"Yes," said Arabella. "Of course. But right now, up here in the air, with all the freedom to touch . . . and home so close below . . . I don't know which way I want to go most."

And by then ZoZo was asleep, and Miss Shrubb said, "Do you think it might be time to go down, just for now?"

"Yes," said Murk. "I guess we'll call it a night."

"But what a night!" said Oggy, and when he had set the fan blades right, he picked up his oboe and piped them back to the cornfield.

16

The Fourth Flight

Morning dawned bright and busy. Arabella asked **Mr. Manoover** for a few particular things. "Do you have anything like a long piece of stiff paper or material?"

"I've got the canvas that I use to shade the young plants in spring," said Mr. Manoover.

"That sounds good," said Arabella. "And we'll give it back. Now, could we borrow a little of that red barn paint and a brush?"

"Why, sure," said Mr. Manoover. "I'll get it for you." And he went off to the barn, with Murk and Oggy going along to help carry things.

"What are we going to do, Arabella?" asked Melinda.

"We are going to prepare some propaganda material," said Arabella, "to support our second request."

Three hours later the Goodbury town square looked like a fair. *Everybody* was there, as if by prearrangement, and an oddly gala spirit prevailed—odd considering the gravity of the matter. And not only the people of Goodbury were there. Newspaper reporters and radio commentators from all the neighboring states and television and newsreel photographers were there in great numbers, in trucks with blaring loudspeakers. Besides these out-of-towners, the Assistant Attorney General had been replaced by the Under-Secretary of the Interior, who, with his entourage of under-under-secretaries, lent a formal air to the occasion. He had been quizzing the Mayor closely on the matter of the marsh, and the Mayor had spent the morning squirming uncomfortably and displaying his usual palette of reddish skin tones. The Mayor had cause to wonder, in the course of the morning, how he could have been so unfortunate as to have arrived, at random, at just that one particular ill-starred idea to achieve popularity. He even began to wonder what was so absolutely marvelous about being mayor at all . . . but he dismissed that thought quickly.

Down in the square, people were forming into sociable knots. Some had brought their lunches in paper bags, and there was a great deal of chatter. Even the parents of the five flying children looked a bit more relaxed. One might say they looked more hopeful than yesterday, though there was a certain underlying anxiety. After all, what *would* the children ask for now?

At exactly one o'clock a child standing in front of the library yelled, "There they are!" There was a communal intake of breath, and then everyone exhaled in unison.

"What *is* that?" asked the man from South Street. "*Now* what are them kids doing?"

"There's some sort of banner or something on that flying machine," the Mayor was saying as he leaned far out his window. (One of the Mayor's advisors found himself with the irrational urge to push the Mayor entirely out the window, but, of course, he was a better politician than that.)

As the tree house came closer to the square, it was possible to see just what that strange banner was draped over the railing on all sides. It was a sort of sign, and the people on the ground read it out loud as it became legible to them . . . this depending on the excellence of their eyesight. Some of the older men, who were getting a little farsighted, were the first to be able to read it. "DON'T-BE-SO-MEAN," the hardware man read slowly, and he looked puzzled.

On the south side of the square, it was possible to read another side of the banner. "DON'T PUSH," read Mr. Kitt. "What *can* they have in mind now?"

On the north side of the square the Under-Secretary of the Interior was reading, "DOWN WITH APATHY. I think there's some mistake here," he said to the Mayor. "This has nothing at all to do with the Department of the Interior."

"What department has it to do with?" asked the Mayor, without much interest.

"I'm not sure we have a department that handles apathy," said the Under-Secretary, "though I confess I'm not sure. But I'll talk to the Secretary of State about it."

On the west side of the square a third-grade boy read the two-word message on the banner, "PAY AT-TENTION." And everyone else on the west side of the square read it in unison. "PAY ATTENTION," everyone said over and over.

"PAY ATTENTION. How strange!" said the dry-goods lady.

The tree house circled the square several times giving everyone a chance to read all sides of the banner. "PAY ATTENTION," the people on the east side of the square now read, while the people on the west side were reading "DON'T BE SO MEAN." "DON'T PUSH," the townspeople on the north side of the square were reading, while the people on the south side were puzzling over DOWN WITH APATHY.

"I guess they've all had a chance to see them now," said Murk. "Shall I put her into hover?"

"Okay," said Arabella, and she came to the front of the platform as Murk and Oggy adjusted the tree house controls to a pleasant hover just in front of the town hall. The Mayor had an excellent view, as did the Under-Secretary of the Interior. "Incredible!" the Under-Secretary kept saying. "Incredible!"

"You'll get used to it," said the Mayor. "Right now, I feel those kids have been running this town for years. I tell you, I'm up to my ears with those kids!"

"Good afternoon," Arabella called through the megaphone, giving a special nod to the Mayor. The rest of the children stood up and waved to their parents and the townspeople.

"Good afternoon," everyone called back.

"For heaven's sake!" Arabella said to the children and Miss Shrubb. "They certainly sound very cheerful," and she turned back to the railing.

"We're back," she said, "as promised. And we want to thank you for doing the right thing yesterday."

And then Miss Shrubb came timidly to the edge of the platform and called, "I want to thank you, too. So much! You have done a very fine thing. A very fine thing." And quite suddenly a flight of geese circled around the town hall and around the tree house. Miss Shrubb pointed. "They are thanking you, too," said Miss Shrubb, and she sat down.

"Extraordinary!" said the Under-Secretary of the Interior.

"Infuriating!" said the Mayor.

Arabella had been looking rather abstracted while Miss Shrubb was speaking. Now she suddenly said into the megaphone, "Do any of you know the exports of Venezuela?"

A great many people looked rather puzzled, and Mr. Serafin said, "What has that got to do with it?"

But the man next to him said, "Say, I bet I still remember the exports of Venezuela."

Mr. Serafin asked one of the television cameramen

if he could use the loudspeaker. "There's a man here who knows them, Arabella. Do you want him to come to the loudspeaker?"

"Okay," said Arabella.

"Hey, Arabella," asked Murk. "What's the sense of it?"

"I don't know," Arabella said, frowning. "It seemed to make sense when I asked it."

The man at the loudspeaker hitched up his trousers, cleared his throat, and began to recite loudly, in a singsong voice. "The chief exports of Venezuela are: petroleum, iron ore, coffee, and cacao."

"That's very good," said Arabella. "When did you learn that?"

"Oh, say twenty years ago," the man said modestly. "Back in seventh grade or so. Stuck in my mind."

"Well, I was just interested," said Arabella, "because we just learned it a few weeks ago. Was it very useful these twenty years?"

"Never thought of it again until this minute," the man said, squirming a bit.

"Arabella," called Mr. Serafin, "where is this getting us? Can't you tell us what it is you want?"

"Come on, Arabella," said Oggy impatiently.

Arabella brought herself back to the matter at hand.

"All right," she said. "We are here now with our second condition. You see, to be quite truthful, we don't expect to be in a position to get what we want again for an awfully long time; and there are so many things we want, and so many things we want to do . . . and we know we can't do all of them so we are trying to do the things that will do the most good." She took a deep breath.

"That's what comes of spoiling kids!" muttered the man from South Street. "Give 'em a fancy flying machine and they think they own the world!"

"Now," Arabella went on, "yesterday all of you together did something so special. Oh, just look at the good that people can do when they want to! But the trouble is . . . everywhere . . . the trouble is that they don't want to . . . enough. Oh, they read about what's happening." Arabella stopped and smiled. "I do that myself. I used to, anyway. They read and they hear what's going on, but they don't *do* anything. And you see, *that's* what we want. We want . . . we want you to . . . to pay attention to what people are doing and saying and . . . and *needing*. We want you to listen to us, to all the children, to the other people in Goodbury, to people all over the country . . . *all over the world!*" Arabella's voice was mounting in pitch and she was gesticulating wildly when she said, "the world." And then she turned back to the children. "Oh, I just can't seem to make it clear. It's because I'm emotionally involved. I'm not at all clever when I'm emotionally involved."

Melinda was hopping about restlessly. "Honestly," she said. "I wish I'd asked for the party dress and shoes. I really wanted them."

"That's because you're feeling selfish," snapped Murk. "You don't *care* enough about it. That's all!" Melinda looked chastened, but Oggy shouted, "That's *it!*" and grabbed the megaphone and called down to the square, "Just *care,* that's all! *Really* care! Everything else can come from that."

"Everything!" shouted Arabella triumphantly as she smiled gratefully at Oggy.

And Murk yelled, "It's just like the marsh, see— we're all tied up together!" And then he sat down, brick red.

There were popping flashes of light around the square where cameramen were at work, and a loudspeaker on one of the newsreel trucks blared. "Hey, kids," the cameraman yelled, "could you fly over here so we can get a better shot of you?"

"Arabella," called Mr. Serafin, "that's all very good

and perfectly sound, but just what shall we *do?*"

"What should they do, do you think, Murk?"

"Gosh," said Murk. "Just talk about it. Think about it . . . like."

Melinda came up and waved to her mother. "Honestly," she said, "it's so easy. Just say you will, that's all."

"And then *do* it," added Arabella, feeling much better as things straightened out. "You must stay in the square for an hour now and talk about it . . . just talk about it. Then tell us on the radio tonight what you think."

"But Arabella," called Mr. Serafin, rather worried. "We *want* to do what you want us to, but it's so vague."

Arabella was exasperated. "We're only trying to make things better," she said a bit snappishly. "We're just asking you to do a few little things to help make it better for everyone. That's all. After all, you're grown-ups. You should be able to figure it out."

"All right," said Mr. Serafin doubtfully. And the other parents looked very worried. "We'll talk about it. Ladies and gentlemen," he said through the loudspeaker, addressing the people in the square. "For a beginning, will you please help us by turning to your neighbor now and starting a discussion of this subject. While it may seem odd, it may help just to begin and see where it leads."

Mrs. Rose was at the loudspeaker as the tree house prepared to leave the square. "Melinda dear," she called. "Are you all right? Do you brush your teeth?"

And before the tree house left, ZoZo came, surprisingly, to the railing and called, "Papa! Papa! When I come down, you let me have white horse? Yes?"

Mr. Sejura said proudly, "He is to be great man. He thinks strongly on one thing." But he shouted into the loudspeaker, "International incident! Outrage!"

The Under-Secretary of the Interior dashed to the phone and called the Under-Secretary of State. "Somebody will have to cool down that man," he said. "It's not a job for Interior."

The bakery man suddenly stood up from his spot on the curb and started to elbow his way through the crowd. "I've been here long enough," he said. "I'm losing business over this."

"Please don't push," said the lady behind him. "Didn't you read the sign? DON'T PUSH, it says."

"I beg your pardon," said the baker, embarrassed. "It's just I'm in a hurry to get back to my shop."

"I'm goin', too," said the man from South Street. "The show's over."

The man beside him said, "Can't you stay and talk awhile, like they asked?"

"Nah!" said the man from South Street. "I'm sick of these spoiled kids. It's got nothing to do with me anyway."

"There!" said the lady from Wisteria Avenue. "*That's* it! It's got nothing to do with you, so you don't want to help."

The man from South Street looked embarrassed. "Aw, come on, lady! What can we do anyway?"

"Look here," said the Wisteria Avenue lady. "These parents are very distressed. Apparently, by just standing here and talking, we can help them somehow. It seems the least we can do. Doesn't it?" she appealed to the baker, who had stopped his retreat.

"How can talk help anything like that?" asked the man from South Street.

"Well," said the lady from Wisteria Avenue, "we did talk that nice little Miss Shrubb back into her marsh yesterday. Talking did that."

"Talked ourselves right out of a racetrack, we did," muttered the man from South Street. But he stayed.

On the other side of the square, the parents were talking among themselves—except for Mr. Sejura, who went to see the Under-Secretary. "I don't know," said Mr. Kitt. "*Don't* we care? I always thought I cared a lot."

"But maybe we just don't care enough about the right things," said Mr. Serafin thoughtfully.

"Like that little Miss Shrubb," said Mrs. Rose. "Poor thing!"

"It was that weak-willed Mayor really," said Mr. Kitt.

"But you voted for him, dear," said Mrs. Kitt.

"Well, because he was the candidate of my party," said Mr. Kitt defensively. "But, yes, by gum, I'll think it over when election time comes around."

Mr. Serafin nodded agreement, and then he said, "Now what was all that about the exports of Venezuela? Did you follow that? I missed the point, somehow. It seemed so trivial."

"But maybe that's it," said Mrs. Serafin. "Maybe Arabella meant it was trivial in view of everything else there is to learn."

"I haven't really looked into the course of study in the school," said Mr. Kitt. "Have any of you?"

Mr. Serafin shook his head. "Arabella's always done so well, I just didn't care much . . ." He smiled.

Talk caught fire around the square, and before long a great many animated conversations were taking place on subjects ranging from garbage disposal to outdoor concerts, politics to flower arranging, medical aid and housing for the poor, and fair labor practices. At least three committees were formed. No one was more surprised than the man from South Street to find himself on a committee, with the lady from Wisteria Avenue, for the purpose of landscaping the town fountain.

There was also a fast game of poker going on near the steps of the town hall, a game of stickball on the green, and an evenly matched fistfight behind the camera truck between two of Goodbury's younger citizens.

"Now you children stop fighting this minute," said an indignant lady. "This minute! Or I shall turn you over to the policeman."

"Don't be so mean," said one of the onlookers.

"Yeah! Don't be so mean!" yelled one of the participants, landing a very effective uppercut.

17

Ready for the Big Deal

That was Tuesday morning. Tuesday night, after an afternoon of sunbathing, clothes washing, and garden chores, the children and Miss Shrubb were joined by Mr. Manoover to listen to the radio, sputtering in the barn.

"No sneezing, please," said Mr. Manoover. "Missus near burned me up with a mustard plaster and choked me with cough syrup the night she came out to the barn and thought it was me sneezing."

"We'll try not to," said Melinda.

"To tell the truth," said Mr. Manoover, "I really fear that Missus is beginning to wonder."

"Wonder?" asked Miss Shrubb.

"Like where are the extra loaves of bread? Like what or who is darting through the vegetable garden?

'Some old dog,' I say, or 'Likely a rabbit,' but she wonders, anyhow."

"Well," said Oggy, "we probably won't be here much longer."

"No," said Murk, almost sadly, "not if they do what we say."

"Actually," said Arabella, "I think, if all goes according to plan, that we should expect to be in our homes tomorrow or the next day."

"I not go," said ZoZo. "I like right here. I not leave white horse."

"You'll have to go, ZoZo," said Melinda. "If we didn't bring you home, we'd be in terrible trouble."

"I not want you to have trouble," said ZoZo. "I go. But I come back," he said to Mr. Manoover.

The radio, which had been grinding out some sour music, much to the distress of Oggy's sensitive ears, now turned to the news of the day. First came bulletins on wars in Asia, an earthquake in Japan, a flood in Brazil. And finally, "There are new developments in the dramatic case of the five flying children who made their third appearance over the town square of Goodbury this morning. Interest in the matter widens as the international implications increase. The Ambassador from Peroque continued his protests as the parents of the children attempted to gain town cooperation for the children's demands.

"In connection with yesterday's action regarding the marsh, the Mayor of Goodbury has characterized it as, quote, 'blackmail,' while the Under-Secretary of the Interior called it, quote, 'extraordinary.' Countrywide approval is reported from conservationists."

"But what about today?" said Arabella impatiently.

As if in response, the announcer said, "In regard to the children's most recent demands, the people of Goodbury held a caucus in the square today, and this bulletin was issued by the parents of the children involved. Quote: 'It is true that people tend to be apathetic. It is a very hard thing to fix in a hurry, but the people of Goodbury will try, at least, not to be apathetic about being apathetic—that is, to care about caring. We agree with the children that *caring* is the key, though, of course, we continue to object to their methods of bringing it to our attention.' End quote.

"Incidental to the caucus on the town square was the formation of several ad hoc committees—one to landscape the town fountain, one to plan a modernization of the course of study at the public schools, one to check on certain town hall activities, and one to investigate living conditions on the south side of town.

"One of the town citizens, Mrs. Amelia Leap of Wisteria Avenue, said, 'It was a most stimulating morning. I felt quite refreshed. I met some very interesting people of a type I have not previously encountered.' Mr. Albert Bugg of South Street said of the informal town meeting, 'Well, I have to admit it turned out different than I thought. At first those kids really got my goat. But then there was this lady—at first I thought she was a busybody, not to mention a snob—but now I think I will decorate the town fountain with her. I am handy around flowers.' End quote. We are informed that the Under-Secretary of State will be arriving in Goodbury tomorrow."

"Aha!" cried Arabella. "Just the right person!"

"Does all this mean," asked Melinda, "that from now on everybody is going to care about *everything* and *everybody?*"

"No," said Arabella. "That would be expecting too much. But I think it means that for the time being, at least, a lot of people's eyes are opened. And then if they start noticing and caring, perhaps . . . perhaps . . ."

"Perhaps," said Miss Shrubb, "some of them may just get in the habit."

"That's it," said Arabella. "And now, we are ready for the *coup de grâce*."

"The what?" asked Murk.

"The big deal," said Arabella.

"I want to ask you something," said Mr. Manoover. "If you all are going to be going away soon, I am wondering if you would let me go with you tomorrow? I have something I would like to say to all those people . . . if I don't lose my nerve."

"Why, sure!" said Oggy, clapping Mr. Manoover on the back. "We'd like it. Wouldn't we, Arabella?"

"Yes," said Arabella. "It would be fine, because after tomorrow it won't matter if they know we are staying here at the farm."

"All right," said Mr. Manoover. "I'll be ready."

"Okay," said Arabella. "Now, let's get busy."

Some of them got busy. ZoZo fell asleep on the back of the white horse.

18

This Has Got to Stop!

The Under-Secretary of the Interior had been replaced by the Under-Secretary of State, who now stood at the window of the Mayor's office. "Have you any idea the commotion this is causing, country-wise?" he asked with annoyance. "It seems to me that a good local administration could have managed this whole thing with more discretion. But no, here I am . . . in a town called Goldbury . . ."

"Goodbury," said the Mayor.

". . . when there are important things happening all over the world that need my attention. We've got a war-and-a-half going, you know."

"I know," said the Mayor. "Believe me," and he started his routine face-mopping, "I find this whole thing quite as inconvenient as you do. Look out there," and he pointed to the crowded square. "There's been scarcely a lick of work done in Goodbury since those kids went up. Look at those people! You'd think it was a national holiday." And then he said, "Oh, heavens! Here they come again!" High over the church steeple the tree house appeared.

As usual, it circled the tower a few times and Oggy rang the church bell. It served the purpose of alerting the people in the square and it was fun. The tree house then flew straight toward the Mayor's window and came to a hover in front of it. The Under-Secretary of State was having trouble maintaining his composure. "My sainted aunt!" he said under his breath.

"Now! You see what we're up against!" the Mayor said with some satisfaction.

"Hallooo," yodeled Arabella through the megaphone.

The Mayor gave a weak nod and flip of his hand. The Under-Secretary only stared.

"If you're the Under-Secretary of State," said Arabella, "I just want to tell you to pay especial attention to what we are going to say, because it has a lot to do with you."

"Me!" exclaimed the Under-Secretary. "Now look

here . . ." But the tree house turned and cruised to its now customary position above the town square.

Everybody waved and threw kisses. A child from Lilac Place set off a few firecrackers and rockets and got a good whack for it, but it was worth it. One of the rockets whizzed right past the tree house, and it was highly dramatic.

Oggy brought them to order with a prolonged "E" on the oboe, and then Arabella took over the megaphone.

"Before we begin the business of the day, I should like to introduce a friend of ours, Mr. Sam Manoover. He will address you briefly."

"Oh, lor'," said Mr. Manoover to Miss Shrubb. "Now I wish I had not come."

"Oh, pshaw!" said Miss Shrubb. "You'll be fine."

So Mr. Manoover shuffled to the railing and, taking the megaphone from Arabella, began his first public oration. His first words were very high-pitched, much to his surprise, so he started again on a lower note of the scale.

"I want to . . . I want to tell you all about this corn here," and he bent down and picked up a large stalk he had brought from his farm. It amazed him to see that everyone's eyes remained fixed on him, and it gave him some courage. He had supposed that as soon as he began to speak everyone would pack up and leave.

"This corn," he continued, holding up the stalk, "is shoe peg . . . shoe peg corn . . . and that's the finest, tastiest, sweetest corn you ever had. Beautiful it is, too, with every little kernel just about the same size as the next, set in straight rows"— Mr. Manoover was being swept up in his own enthusiasm—"the whole thing shining like a real good set of teeth. That corn," he said, shaking the stalk at them, "that corn is what I call CORN. All right, what I want to tell you is . . . you know who grows that corn? I do. I, Sam Manoover. I grow that corn. And when you go into the vegetable store and pick up an ear of that fine corn, don't forget who grew it for you. I did. Sam Manoover."

Mr. Manoover sat down, feeling at once fulfilled and empty. "Ahhh," he said to anyone who might hear, "it doesn't matter. Now I've done it, but it doesn't matter. I get more of a kick out of growing that corn than I do out of telling them about it. But that's some beautiful corn . . . beautiful . . . even if I'm the only one to know it. Yup!"

Miss Shrubb reached over and took the corn from him. "Why, look at those lovely little kernels," she said. "They look like pearls. Beautiful!"

Mr. Manoover turned pink. "Please to keep it," he said. "I would like you to have it. A remembrance."

Miss Shrubb smiled with pleasure. "I thank you," she said. "I thank you kindly."

In the square the reaction was one of restrained interest. A few polite nods were exchanged and a few eyebrows raised. But one lady, alone, reacted strongly. She had come to the square late, and it was her first visit this week. A neighbor had stopped by, told her about the goings-on, and given her a lift. They had arrived at the square in time to see Mr. Manoover first wave the ear of corn. They had listened, open-mouthed, and then the lady had cried, *"That's Samuel Manoover! My Sam Manoover!"* She poked the man next to her. "That's my husband, Sam Manoover," she said, scarcely believing it herself, suddenly, and for the first time, quite proud. "That Sam Manoover," she said to everyone around, "grows the tallest, sweetest corn in the world. He's telling the *truth.*"

Now Arabella came to the railing again, Oggy blew her a nice bright tattoo on the oboe, and everyone came to attention. Arabella seemed a bit nervous. "We got your message about yesterday," she said, "and so we're back. And it seems to us, if you all do things the way you did yesterday and the day before, you can fix anything you want to . . . if . . ."

"If you *want* to," shouted Murk.

"Yes," said Arabella. "If you want to. And so today we are going to ask you the last thing, and then we will come down."

"Well, thank heaven for that," said the Mayor. "It's probably just some more talk, and talk is cheap."

"Hush," said the Under-Secretary, who was fascinated. "Just look at the way the people are paying attention to her!"

And then suddenly everyone on the tree house started to throw down some little floating things into the square, and the Mayor caught one as it went by. The people were scrambling about picking them up or catching them as they fell.

"Why, it's a little piece of corn husk," said the Mayor, turning it over in his hand.

"But there's something painted on it," said the Under-Secretary. "What does it say?"

"PEACE," read the Mayor. "That's all it says . . . PEACE."

"PEACE," read the man from South Street. "PEACE," read the lady from Wisteria Avenue. "PEACE," read the boy with the firecrackers. "PEACE," read the baker and the hardware man.

"PEACE," read Mr. Serafin and Mr. Rose.

"PEACE," read the Ambassador from Peroque.

Arabella spoke into the megaphone. Her voice shook a bit, but she said strongly, "Peace. That's what we want now. Peace in the world." She turned to the Under-Secretary of State. "You must stop the wars."

"Stop the wars?" cried the Under-Secretary.

"You must stop the wars, and then we will come down."

In the square the people were confused. "I'm for that," said the hardware man. "But how are they going to do it?"

The man from South Street said, "Now, just when I was softening up on them kids! Stop the wars!"

Arabella was getting very excited. Her eyes were burning and she breathed rapidly. "Just pick up the telephone." Her voice was rising. "Call the President. Tell him to stop the wars, or we shall fly off and never come back." And now her hands flew up to cover her eyes.

"Arabella!" cautioned Miss Shrubb softly, but Arabella was beginning to sob.

"You tell him we shall fly off with the Ambassador's son," Arabella cried, "and *then* he will have some trouble. You tell him . . . *this has got to stop!*"

Miss Shrubb came over and put her arm around her. "You come and sit down for a minute, Arabella."

"Oh, Arabella!" pleaded Melinda. "*You* mustn't cry!" Whereupon Melinda began to sob.

The three boys stood by uncomfortably and Murk said, "There's something wrong."

Arabella was fighting her tears now, taking deep breaths. It was a gallant and partially successful effort. "It's that I got emotionally involved again," she sobbed between gulps of breath. "Oh, what am I going to do? I just can't think clearly when I'm emotionally in-

volved. I read all about the Roman Empire, all about Greece, all about the Turks and the Egyptians, all about *everything,* and I didn't get emotionally involved . . . and *they* were all at war."

"Living is more emotional than reading," said Miss Shrubb as Oggy brought Arabella a drink of water from the cooler.

The people in the square were forming into groups again, talking it over. The parents were terribly concerned. Mrs. Rose began to cry. "Oh, dear," she said. "*How* are we going to get those children down?"

"There, there," soothed Mr. Rose, without much conviction, and he looked rather worried himself.

The Under-Secretary looked very pensive and started to pace around the Mayor's office. "But this is very important!" he said. "Much more important than I was led to believe. These children are telling us that they disapprove of us. I told my father the same thing."

The Mayor, turning to his deep purple now, yelled out the window, "Blackmailers! Blackmailers!"

Oggy heard him and said, "The Mayor is calling us blackmailers."

"Ah, him!" said Mr. Manoover, who had been quietly nibbling on an ear of corn.

"Well, we are," said Murk, unabashedly. "Sure, we are."

Mr. Manoover looked surprised. "Well, now!" he said, thinking it over. "Well, now!" And then he asked, "Do you really think they can do that—stop the wars?"

Murk said, "Well, we figured if the Under-Secretary wouldn't do it, we could get everyone to follow the tree house and we could lead a big parade to Washington, with everyone joining in behind, and we could just tell the President. That's all."

"That's all!" breathed Miss Shrubb. Arabella's sobs and gulps were less frequent and hard now, but every few seconds she shuddered and shook her head.

Mr. Manoover sat on the bench, distressfully regarding Arabella's distress. Finally he said, "I'm a farmer, you know, but I've noticed some things. And one thing I noticed, when I was only a boy, was that my father was making nothing out of our farm. He would not let any of the fields rest, he would not plow in contours, he would not rotate. No! 'Do it like this,' I would say to him. 'Plant this,' I would say to him. No! In the end, when I got big enough, I had to do it myself. The only way was to do it myself. And now look at that corn!"

Miss Shrubb asked softly. "Arabella, what are you thinking?"

Arabella raised her tear-stained face and said quietly, "These days, flying around, it seemed so possible. Being up here, I felt I could look down and see everything so clearly . . . just like in a history book. And then, in the back of my mind, I guess I just had the idea that, if it didn't work and if they wouldn't or couldn't do it, we could really fly somewhere and start something perfect for ourselves, if we had to. But now . . ."

"But now?" asked Miss Shrubb.

"But now"—Arabella stood up and looked at each of the other children in turn—"*I wonder.*"

19

The Decision

The Under-Secretary of State was still in a confused and bemused state during the hiatus in the proceedings. "How wonderful!" he said to the Mayor, "to be young enough to find things so clear and so simple. How wonderful it would be if I *could* do just that—pick up the phone and say, 'Stop the wars!' as if there were not thousands of things standing in the way—rights, wrongs, truths, untruths, politics, confusions, years of history—everything that makes things the way they are. How wonderful to have eyes young enough to see past all that! Perhaps we should turn the country over to the children!"

The Mayor growled, and gestured to the tree house. "We've sure turned the town over to them!"

"And you're none the worse for it, I can see," said the Under-Secretary, suddenly getting up purposefully and walking over to the window. "Children," he called. "Can you hear me?"

The children, who had been talking things out at great length, now turned and nodded.

"My dear children," said the Under-Secretary. "I came here today full of irritation. But now I am glad I came. It will be nice to think, as I grow older, that you are here growing up. But, children, I can't do what you ask."

"We know," said Arabella, red-eyed now but composed. "We've been thinking it over. Words . . . just words aren't enough, are they? There's too much else."

The Under-Secretary nodded. "Much too much," he said.

Arabella was shaking her head. "What can we do?" she asked softly, almost to herself. "What can we do?"

"Look!" the Under-Secretary said. "The things you have done are on the right track, you know. You are right to be thinking about what we in charge are doing with your world. You are right to be talking about it, questioning it . . . yes, even shouting about it. But, no, it's just not going to be enough."

"No," said Murk. "We know that now."

"And when you think about it," the Under-Secretary said a bit more sharply, "flying around in the sky is not the way to get a great deal done, anyhow. Oh, you're getting some attention, but *that's* just not going to do the job." He softened his tone. "Come down," he said. "Come down and *help*. We need you . . . a lot."

There was a quick vote, then, on the tree house, in the sky, over the square of the town of Goodbury. Then Arabella turned back to the Under-Secretary and said, with the old assurance, "All right, then! If *you* can't do it, it looks as though we will just have to come down there and *try to take care of it ourselves.*"

The Under-Secretary clapped his hands together and called down into the square, "Where's that boy with the firecrackers?" The boy from Lilac Place hid behind the fruit cart. "Come on!" cried the Under-Secretary. "Let's have a really good rocket or something, if you have any left. These children are coming down now, and I may add, your town is wonderfully lucky to have them!"

The square erupted in applause, and suddenly a pink and green rocket flew up toward the church tower and exploded into a star.

20

. . . And What Happened Then?

The tree house circled the town hall, and everyone waved, the parents all wept happy tears, and the towns-people cheered. It was a first-class occasion. Then the tree house flew off over the town, across the river, over the little woods, and out over the marsh. Then it went into its descent . . . slowly, slowly . . . right over Miss Shrubb's little house, and Murk put the craft into a hover and threw over the rope ladder. Miss Shrubb, wearing all her skirts and sweaters and clutching the souvenir ear of corn, bid her adieus and warm invitations to visit. Then she went over the side and climbed down the rope ladder right into her own postage-stamp front yard, where she was enthusiastically greeted by a gaggle of geese.

The next hovering stop was over the cornfield. Mr. Manoover, who was very sorry to part from them, did a neat jump into a haystack, and ZoZo called down a promise to come during his vacations to ride the white horse. Everyone joined in calling thank you and promised to visit soon.

Mrs. Manoover was back in time to greet him. "Sam Manoover!" she cried. "How come you never told me about all this?"

"But I did!" protested Mr. Manoover. "Last Saturday I told you about that thing flying over the orchard. Remember?"

"Well!" said Mrs. Manoover, her indignant self again. "You certainly didn't expect me to believe a story like that!"

And then, the final flight over the orchard, over the woods, across the river, over the meadow, and into the Clays' back yard, where pairs of eager parents were standing, heads tipped up, eyes shining, arms extended to embrace the returning travelers.

Oggy and Murk, with the rarest and best of aeronautic skills, slowly, ever so slowly, guided the tree house down . . . hover . . . hover . . . forward a little . . . back a bit . . . down . . . hover . . . until it was set perfectly on the tree stump it had left five days before.

And Melinda said, as Oggy and Murk were congratulating each other, "It's just as though we'd never been away."

And Arabella said, "No, not quite."